# MARION AND THE FORTY THIEVES

*To my Dad,*
*and my friend Robyn*

# Marion and the Forty Thieves

SARAH LUKE
MARTINA HEIDUCZEK

CELEBRATING
NATIONAL LIBRARY OF AUSTRALIA PUBLISHING
OVER 50 YEARS

Published by National Library of Australia Publishing
Canberra ACT 2600

ISBN: 9781922507679



The National Library of Australia acknowledges Australia's First Nations Peoples—the First Australians—as the Traditional Owners and Custodians of this land and gives respect to the Elders—past and present—and through them to all Australian Aboriginal and Torres Strait Islander people.



Publisher: Lauren Smith
Managing editor: Amelia Hartney
Editor: Dr Stephanie Owen Reeder
Designer: Hannah Janzen
Image coordinator: Madeleine Warburton
Printed in China by Everbest Printing Co. Ltd on FSC®-certified paper

Teachers' notes for this book are available at publishing.nla.gov.au/pages/teachers-notes.do.

Find out more about NLA Publishing at nla.gov.au/national-library-publishing.

NATIONAL LIBRARY OF AUSTRALIA
A catalogue record for this book is available from the National Library of Australia

FSC www.fsc.org
MIX
Paper from responsible sources
FSC® C124385

## CHAPTER 1

# THE LOONG SHAN TEA HOUSE

Marion leant forward, carefully considering the menu before her. She was sitting opposite her mother at a white-clothed table.

Marion eyed the list of delicacies. She and her mother had arrived for afternoon tea, and Marion was glad she could skip the main luncheon courses—boiled ham, corned beef and carrots, mock turtle soup, and something *terrible* called jugged hare! Her eyes drifted down the list of delicious cakes and pastries—apple pies with custard, plum puddings, apricot rolls, lemon ices and sponge cakes.

She sighed. She knew her mother would order scones for them both to enjoy. They were the speciality of the

Loong Shan Tea House in Sydney, owned by businessman Mr Quong Tart. His famous scones were advertised on the specials board on the wall opposite. The blackboard had a thick golden frame. Marion admired the beautiful copperplate handwriting. She wished hers was so regular and grown-up. At the bottom of the board was an advertisement for a new favourite on the menu: 'Latest Iced Fountain Drinks! Lemon! Chocolate! Lime! Strawberry!'

Marion licked her lips and regarded her elegant mother. Her hair was pulled neatly back in a bun on top of her head. Her navy-blue dress was secured at the neck by a pretty silver brooch. Her hands rested in her lap, and her elbows were definitely *not* on the table.

Marion's mother was wary of new things. Last year, when she'd taken Marion shopping at a big department store, they'd looked at dress after dress, hat after hat, but none of the new styles had been acceptable to her mother. And even though her mother *said* that Marion may choose, of course she'd not *really* been allowed to. Marion smoothed out her rather drab dress—*that* dress, in fact—and sighed again.

Smartly dressed waitresses in black frocks and frilly white

aprons buzzed around the dining saloon, ferrying dishes to the diners. One stopped at their table.

'Good afternoon, madam, what can I get you?' the young woman asked. She had a kind face, with tiny wrinkles around her eyes and lips, which showed that she smiled often.

Putting aside the menu, Marion's mother announced, 'My daughter and I will have the scones, please, and a pot of tea for two.'

'May-I-have-one-of-the-latest-iced-fountain-drinks-please, Mama?' Marion blurted out, hoping that having an audience might help her case. She could see the glorious soda machine gleaming on the counter, its silver nozzles, tall glasses and long spoons sparkling in the lamplight.

Her mother shifted in her seat, making her corsets creak. She pursed her lips while she considered her daughter—small, eager and neat, with a dark plait hanging down her back.

She paused. She smiled. And then, much to Marion's surprise, she *nodded*. 'Just this once,' she said.

The waitress, also smiling, enquired of the flavour.

'Strawberry, please!'

Thrilled that her mother had relented in her crusade of never letting her try new things, Marion reflected that she should have tried the same trick at the department store last year. She thanked her mother when the waitress had left.

'It's to make up for Agnes leaving for France,' her mother said. 'But don't tell your father.' She winked and began rummaging in her handbag.

Marion peered around the saloon to distract herself from thoughts of her best friend Agnes. From where she was seated, she had an excellent view of the ladies' dining room. It was on the first floor of the tea house, above the men's floor. On the top floor, parties and wedding breakfasts were held. Today, that room was occupied by a group of imperious-looking ladies with severe faces and mahogany canes who were talking loudly about women's suffrage. Marion didn't know what that meant. When she asked, her mother reminded her that she was *only* twelve years old and insisted that she sit down at the table rather than investigate the interesting women.

The dining saloon was busy, filled with women and girls enjoying their food. Over the chatter and the clinking of cutlery and chiming of cups on saucers came the sound of a marble fountain splashing water into a large pool. It was filled with golden carp that shimmered through the water, chasing each other.

A curiously dressed man emerged from a fernery at one end of the room. He scattered food for the fish and then smoothed down his traditional Mandarin robes. Marion admired the wide sleeves, the elegant silk fabric and the minute buttons.

'*That*,' said her mother, 'is Mr Quong Tart himself. He is a great admirer of your father's work, you know. Now do sit up straight, dear.'

The Loong Shan Tea House stood proudly on King Street, shoulder to shoulder with coffee houses, milliners shops and dressmaking studios. Outside, many people were already making their way home after a long day at work. There were clerks in suits, with papers under their arms and harried looks on their faces. Rose-scented women with large hats tugged fussing children behind them. Businessmen smelling of tobacco strolled along with their colleagues, pointing out the sights with their walking sticks.

Ragged children, lowly members of Sydney's gangs, were crawling out of their hiding places, ready for the evening's hijinks. Some of the street urchins begged for spare coins or food from the clerks in their suits, the rose-scented women and the businessmen with their canes. Others charmed coins from pockets with their light fingers when the clerks, women and businessmen weren't watching.

Further down King Street, a boy was turning somersaults in the air, hoping to earn money by impressing his audience. Beside him, a girl juggled three dull-coloured balls. Other homeless children meandered across the street, getting in the way of vehicles and pedestrians alike.

Safe inside the tearooms, Marion sat straight in her seat watching as Quong Tart stopped at the counter and asked something of their waitress. She nodded in their direction. In an instant, Quong Tart himself was at their table holding a heavy tray.

'Mrs Neitenstein,' he began, bowing deeply to her mother

and doffing his square cap, while carefully balancing the tray without upsetting the drinks.

Marion's mother inclined her head. 'Allow me to introduce my daughter, Marion. She has been here several times before, but I don't think you have ever met.'

'Miss Neitenstein,' Mr Tart replied, bowing grandly and lifting his cap again.

'You pronounce our family name—"Nay-ten-shtain"—very well,' said Marion, as Mr Tart set down their drinks with a flourish.

Mr Tart put a tall glass filled to the brim with bubbling soda in front of Marion, then gestured to it like a magician who had magicked a rabbit from a top hat.

'It's such a tricky name to say,' Marion continued. 'It's European, you know, and so most of the boys on the ship call my father 'Dutchy' instead.'

Mr Tart chuckled, but her mother frowned.

'But not to his face,' Marion quickly added.

Mr Tart stroked an imaginary beard on his clean-shaven chin and continued. 'As you say, Miss Neitenstein, names can be tricky.' He held a finger in the air. 'Your story puts me in mind of a lady who came here some years ago when my luncheon rooms were new. Having heard of the famous "Quong Tart", she assumed it was an item on the menu. After finishing her oyster soup, she requested that the waitress bring her a Quong Tart to finish her meal. My staff came to me, fearing a complaint, only to discover the confusion between myself'—he stamped his foot dramatically like a flamenco dancer—'and a *pastry*!' He traced his profile with a dancer-like gesture and added, 'We are quite different, I am sure you will agree!'

After presenting their scones with a flourish, Mr Tart bid them good day and moved on to another table, where he danced a Scottish jig, much to the amusement of an elderly lady.

Marion's mother poured them both a cup of tea from a large pastel-coloured teapot decorated with leaves, flowers and traditional scenes from Mr Tart's home country, China. Then she offered Marion first choice from the plate of scones and jam.

Outside the tearooms, King Street was crawling with street

urchins, some of whom were working. A grubby young street-sweeper was tempting coins from passing businessmen. Nearby, a brother and sister in ragged clothes polished shoes on the side of the street, borrowing space under the awning of a grocery shop. They cast suspicious glances around them as they polished and buffed.

A few shops down from them, a rough-looking boy approached a small lad selling newspapers. Without a pause, the big boy punched the newspaper boy in the stomach. He doubled-over, gasping, and coins spilled from his pockets. A gaggle of young girls dashed out from their hiding place in the alley opposite, scooped up the coins in their ragged skirts, and skittered away on bare feet.

'Mr Tart is very generous with his time and his catering,' Mrs Neitenstein told her daughter in the cosy atmosphere of the tearooms. Marion nodded as she spooned raspberry jam onto her plate and took up her butterknife. 'He holds parties for the poor and the neglected here in Sydney, and he plans to bring the

*Sobraon* boys here as soon as your father can arrange it.'

Marion wasn't sure what the boys under her father's command would make of Mr Tart's exotic tearooms. She peered around, trying to imagine three hundred boys in sailor suits crammed into the tiny space. In contrast, the Nautical School Ship *Sobraon*, which her father was captain and principal of, was huge, with its library, dormitory, mess room and classrooms.

She took a bite of her scone. It was dense and warm, the jam thick and sweet, and the iced soda was deliciously fizzy. The food made her think of her friend Agnes, who right now was probably enjoying tea on the deck of the *Wardley* as she sailed away from Sydney, back to England, and then on to France to stay with her aunt. Marion hoped Agnes was still wearing the gold pendant that matched her own. They had gifted them to each other. Marion was certainly wearing hers.

Mother and daughter sat in silence for most of the meal. Mrs Neitenstein occasionally pointed out things of interest in the dining saloon, while Marion spent most of the time thinking about Agnes.

When Marion's mother tried to pay for their afternoon tea,

Mr Tart would not hear of taking her money. He even wrapped up a box of his finest Loong Shan Congou tea for her to take home.

'Madam,' he told her, 'your husband works night and day. You live on a school ship with three hundred neglected and orphaned boys, and you have no garden of your own! Allow me to give this to you on behalf of the colony of New South Wales.' He paused, hands resting on the counter, and then burst forth:

*Some hae meat and canna eat,*
*And some wad eat that want it,*
*But we hae meat, and we can eat,*
*Sae let the Lord be thankit.*

Marion's mother nodded solemnly. 'Ah, the great Scottish bard,' she said.

Marion looked from one to the other, but neither Mr Tart nor her mother explained who the poet was.

As mother and daughter moved down the stairs into the smoke-filled atmosphere of the men's level of the tearooms, Marion reflected on what Mr Tart had said. They did indeed live with three hundred boys onboard the *Sobraon*. But they definitely had a garden—it was called Cockatoo Island.

The *Sobraon* had towering masts and dozens of portholes along the water's edge. Two massive anchors kept it securely chained to the floor of the Parramatta River so it never sailed anywhere.

Marion's father was in charge of a dozen staff, who helped him run the floating boarding school. The boys spent their days doing school lessons and looking after the ship. As Captain Neitenstein's family, Marion and her mother lived onboard, in a special apartment in the stern of the ship.

Mr Tart led the two of them through the men's parlour—a sea of black coats, round spectacles and bald heads—opened the door for them with a flourish and bid them good day. As they stepped out onto King Street, Marion settled her hat on her head and pulled her plait over her shoulder.

She did not notice the many pairs of ravenous eyes staring out from alleyways and dark doorways, and from behind barrows, which were now fixed on her every move.

CHAPTER 2

# AMONG THIEVES

The sun was setting and King Street was busy. Nearby, a young acrobat somersaulted along the pavement and a girl about Marion's age juggled balls above her head. Marion wished she had their freedom. Even the boys on the *Sobraon* had more adventures than she did. After spending a year onboard the floating school, they were sent off to farms to learn how to milk cows, ride horses and harvest crops. The most she could look forward to was dress fittings and invitations to boring social gatherings with her parents.

Her mother seized her hand, and they moved quickly from under the awning of Quong Tart's tearooms and set off along King Street. They were heading for the Circular Quay.

'Look, Mama!' Marion urged, tugging at her mother's hand.

They watched as a boy sauntered up to a sweaty tradesman. The man was struggling to deliver a heavy box to a butcher's shop a few doors down from Quong Tart's tearooms. The sauntering boy was Marion's age, with a scowl on his face and bruised ankles peeking out under fraying trousers. His toes had burrowed holes in his shoes. He spat on the pavement, scratched his head, stuffed his hands in his pockets and approached the tradesman.

Marion's mother tightened her grip on her daughter's hand. 'A perfect boy for your father's school,' she said, nodding at the lad, who was now crossing the road and coming towards them. 'Probably an orphan with no one to help him but the captain of a local push,' she said rather contemptuously.

'Isn't it good if the leader of one of the gangs helps him?' Marion asked. The boy was now leaning against a wall, hands still in his pockets, watching the tradesman closely.

'Not if it's a gang leader,' her mother told her. 'The push captain makes his followers steal for him. He feeds them in return, of course, but they eventually end up in gaol—the police always catch them.'

Marion shivered. She had seen Darlinghurst Gaol once on a cab ride through that part of the city. It was a fortress, with a great iron door in the centre of a massive stone wall. On the other side of that wall were men and women who'd been found guilty of terrible crimes. Some of them were hanged in there.

Marion's mother stopped and burrowed into her handbag. Marion watched as the juggler's balls spun through the air nearby. She wished she knew how to juggle.

'If they're arrested before they do something terrible,' Marion's mother went on, 'they're sent to your father and saved from the streets. They become tailors, farmers and carpenters, not con artists and burglars.'

'Evenin', sir,' Marion heard the boy say casually to the tradesman, who was now sitting on the box he was meant to be carrying and wiping his sweaty face with a handkerchief. 'Feelin' the collar, eh? It's a warm evenin', it's true.'

The tradesman ignored him like people ignore skittish stray dogs they're afraid of. Watching the boy warily out of the corner of his eye, he heaved himself up, lifted the box and shuffled towards an open door nearby.

The lad edged closer, flicking his wrist in what looked like a signal. Sure enough, three boys sloped out of the shadows from the other side of the street. Like the first boy, they were covered in dirt and wore ragged clothing.

As the three sauntered across the street, they collided with the acrobat and the juggler. A rat-faced boy pushed the girl with his hand, without even looking at her, and she fell backwards, her juggling balls rolling off in three directions. Before she could cry out, the boy flashed a blade at her. She didn't resist as he stuffed his hand into her apron pocket and pulled out several coins. Once the boy had moved on, the acrobat ran over, a look of terror on his face. He pulled the girl up, and hand in hand they pelted off down the nearest alleyway.

Nearby, the tall boy was still talking to the tradesman. 'I get it. You think this is some kind of fit-up, don't you? A hawk 'n' pigeon situation, like?' The boy gestured to himself and then to the big-bellied, stubby-legged man.

The tradesman tried to elbow the lad out of the way. 'Get goin', you larrikin, before I call the police,' he growled.

The boy was joined by his three bottle-shouldered companions. A few passers-by, sensing danger, crossed to the other side of the road, tut-tutting and re-adjusting their hats and coats. An empty space soon encircled the tradesman and the vicious boys as the passers-by hurried off, muttering to one another.

'Gangs everywhere in Sydney these days,' one said.

'Those homeless boys are uncontrollable. Send them all to the *Sobraon*!' said another.

Marion was keen to move away too, but her mother was still searching for something in her bag.

'He got any grey on him?' one boy asked, rubbing his thumb and fingers together to indicate money.

Before he could answer, a blonde boy strode towards the group, swaggering along as though he owned the very road upon which he walked. The other boys stopped dead.

'Too much talk,' the newcomer announced, and the others fell silent. 'Cheese 'n' crust! It's broad daylight. The black maria'll be here any minute,' he snarled.

Marion listened for the sound of the police van, but she heard nothing. Then, without warning, the blonde boy lunged at the tradesman. There was a yelp as the man was caught around the neck in a headlock, and a clatter as the box he was holding shuddered to the ground.

Marion's mother looked up and snapped her bag shut. The rat-faced boy who had knocked the juggler down spied Marion and her mother. With a wicked look towards the handbag and the package of tea from Mr Tart, he loped towards them. But a call went up from the blonde boy, and the rat-faced boy turned back.

The blonde boy shook his head vigorously and pointed in Marion's direction. 'That's Dutchy's wife and kid,' he called out. 'Leave 'em be. Bragg'll handle 'em in time.'

Just then, an all-out brawl began.

The blonde boy yelled out to one of the others, 'Filch the redding!' as he ripped the tradesman's watch from his waistcoat pocket and made to throw it to a runner.

'It's the Forty Thieves push. Help! Thieves!' the tradesman cried. The blonde boy held on to the watch as police whistles sounded from a side street and people scattered out of the way. Then a new gang of roughs arrived.

'Blimey! The King Mob push are here!' someone yelled as the Forty Thieves boys were set upon.

'Long way from your patch, aren't you?' one of the King Mob boys yelled. 'I'll teach you to come this far up the city!'

They fought one-on-one as they tried to evade the police by scattering down the alleyways. The shrill sound of police whistles reverberated down the street.

When the scene cleared, just one boy was left—the blonde boy from the Forty Thieves. He lay deadly still on the ground, the stolen watch in his outstretched hand. A bruise was forming on his temple and the tradesman's booted foot was triumphantly planted on the boy's chest.

# CHAPTER 3
# THE NAUTICAL SCHOOL SHIP *SOBRAON*

Marion wanted to watch the blonde boy being bundled into the police van, but her mother would not hear of it. She led her along Castlereagh Street down to the Circular Quay, where a small cutter was tethered to a wharf on the north edge of the harbour.

A crew of boys in neat sailor suits awaited them. They had anchor badges sewn on their left sleeves, identifying them as prefects from the Nautical School Ship *Sobraon*. They alone were trusted to convey the captain's family to and from the ship, and to go on errands in the city.

As soon as mother and daughter were spotted, the boys stood to attention, saluting them. One boy sprang out of the vessel and helped Mrs Neitenstein safely into her seat on the shifting boat. A group of passing dockworkers stopped to watch, arms folded and pipes hanging from between their lips.

'I'm sorry we're late, Williams,' Marion's mother said as she shifted along to make room for Marion and settled her long skirts around her on the bench. The little boat wobbled as she moved. 'There was quite a scene on King Street. The Forty Thieves were fighting the King Mob and trying to beat up a tradesman. The man is a little worse for wear, but he made a citizen's arrest on one of the thieves.'

Williams nodded politely to Marion's mother. As usual, the boys greeted Marion with just a nod in her general direction rather than the smiles and steadying hands they offered to her mother. Marion stepped off the wharf and onto the boat unassisted. She almost toppled over as the vessel lurched in the water when the wake of a ship hit it.

'Will the thief be brought on board soon, ma'am?' asked Williams, leaving Marion to make her own way to the space beside her mother.

At Williams' signal, a boy coiled up the rope attached to the wharf and stowed it neatly behind him.

Her mother resumed the conversation. 'Certainly, the thief might be brought to the *Sobraon*,' she replied.

'He'll not like the idea at first,' said a freckle-faced boy beside Williams. 'Boys in the gangs are taught to fear our ship.'

'Of course they are,' Marion's mother replied, setting her handbag on her lap.

'The Forty Thieves were a long way from home on King Street,' another of the prefects said, thinking out loud.

A look from Williams silenced him. 'We all know about your old life, Bell. You would do well to forget it yourself.'

Marion had heard Williams speak to his fellow prefects in this way before. He was to receive a handsome silver half-hunter pocket watch on his graduation from the ship in a few months' time as the prize for being the most popular prefect. Marion thought him terribly bossy, and the promise of the prize had not helped matters. She rolled her eyes, safe in the knowledge that the boys never even looked in her direction.

'We are none of us tethered to our past, boys,' Mrs Neitenstein proclaimed in the voice she usually reserved for lecturing Marion about deportment and good manners. 'You boys have done well on the *Sobraon*. You have learned your lessons and are almost ready for the next stage of your lives.' She turned to another of the boys. 'Speaking of which, do you have news of your apprenticeship, George?'

George, a gangly boy of about fifteen, flushed bright red at being spoken to directly. 'Yes, ma'am. I'm going up to Singleton to be near my sister and work on a dairy farm. The captain says I can expect to go up in the new year.'

'Good,' was the brisk reply. 'Now, off we go.'

Marion loved the trip from the Circular Quay to the *Sobraon*. The boys rowed the cutter through the water, dodging past steamers and ferries. The salty air whipped through her hair, pulling some of it out of the plait that dangled down her back. She held onto her hat as they ploughed out of the Quay, past Dawes Point Battery and The Rocks, Millers Point with its old warehouses, and Goat Island, towards the Parramatta River.

The waterways were busy today with working ships and pleasure-craft. Before long, Cockatoo Island reared before them. The island was dotted with gardens and a playing field. It was also equipped with a cricket pitch and gymnasium, all under the care of the *Sobraon* boys. The rest of the island was used as a drydock, where ships were brought for maintenance. The island was crowned with the remains of a convict gaol. The boys were not allowed up there, and neither, of course, was Marion.

The magnificent ship *Sobraon* was anchored beside the island, a grand old lady swaying gently on the waves. Sailor-suited boys rushed about cleaning the decks, while men in naval uniforms watched on sternly, occasionally pointing out further work to be done. Other boys were up in the rigging, checking the rope-work or working in teams hauling up the rowboats for the night.

It was almost five o'clock in the evening and soon the boys would be falling in for tea. Then they'd have recreation time until the muster of the ship's company at half-past seven. After that it was prayers and off to bed in their hammocks.

Marion was second up the gangway after her mother, who moved gracefully before her, her long skirts swishing. Marion's father, the captain, was nowhere to be seen. He was probably on the other side of the ship. Marion headed aft to her family's private quarters in the stern. The trip on the cutter had reminded her again of her friend Agnes, now *many* miles away from her, and she wanted to be alone.

Marion was very fond of her bedroom. It was her sanctuary, and she'd been allowed to decorate it as she chose. Beside her bed, which was covered with a quilt made by her aunt, she had a small bookshelf where she stored the books she borrowed from the ship's library. She would have liked to have had books of her own, but Marion was satisfied with the school's large collection.

On the walls were pictures she had painted—mainly views of the harbour and Cockatoo Island, but also some from her imagination, including vistas of jungles and swamps and the animals found there.

Kerosene lamps lit the space. Over the curtained porthole hung a net she had knitted, following instructions she'd found in *The Boy's Own Bookshelf: Indoor Games and Recreations.* It was a fishing net, but it held her dolls off the floor very well indeed.

Up on deck, the bugle sounded, calling the boys to muster for tea. There was the sound of footsteps and much chatter. Then silence descended as the pupils awaited the call to march to the mess room for their meal. Her father preferred to eat with the boys first, so Marion and her mother would have their dinner later when he was free.

To fill in the time, Marion picked up the pile of books she'd finished reading—*The Confessions of Wavering Worthy*, *Twenty Thousand Leagues Under the Sea* and *Kidnapped on the Waves*—and wandered down to the library to exchange them for new ones.

The assistant schoolmaster, Mr Leer, was in the library. Perched on the top rung of a ladder, he was reshelving books and making things tidy. Mr Leer was very young, and very keen. Marion thought he must find it boring teaching the alphabet to boys who were fifteen or sixteen and couldn't write their own names because they'd never been to school. But not all the pupils were like that. Mr Leer also taught history, geography and manual arts, where the boys learnt to make things out of paper and wood.

'Ah! Miss Neitenstein,' he cried as soon as he heard her footsteps at the threshold of the library. He was balancing several books in his hands, so he did not look around, but he began chanting, '*Amo, amas, amat*—'

To which Marion replied, '*Amamus, amatis, amant.*'

Mr Leer slid the books into place and applauded. 'Bravo. You have been studying your Latin. Good girl!'

He jumped down and stepped into the light, away from the shelf he'd been rearranging. He had a pockmarked face and bright eyes shining behind round spectacles. He smiled at Marion. 'Now the boys have gone to tea, you have just under an hour with the collection entirely to yourself.'

Marion shifted her stack of books into Mr Leer's waiting arms and combed the shelves, looking for appealing titles. She preferred to let the books catch her attention. She liked to believe that books *wanted* her to read them and would make themselves known through their covers or titles. Of course, she would never mention this to her father, as he would surely lecture her on the perils of so judging a book.

She skipped over the small selection of books aimed squarely at girls. They had articles about how to decorate a hat or embroider initials onto a lace handkerchief. Marion wasn't very good at sewing and she had little interest in fashion. The books also reminded her of Agnes, who liked that sort of thing.

Marion found some recent editions of the *Boy's Own Annual*—huge cloth-bound volumes with gold-leaf lettering. They were well-thumbed by the pupils whose good behaviour granted them access to the library. In one, she found an interesting article about ventriloquism, and in another a set of instructions for creating a code out of ink-blurs. She sat there for some time, skimming over the other pages, and deciding which books she would borrow. When she'd finished, she told Mr Leer she was heading back to her room to read before dinner with her mother and father.

Mr Leer frowned at her. 'Shouldn't you go to the island with the boys to play?' he asked. He glanced out the porthole nearest to him. 'I'm sure cook could make you up a sandwich for later. I know your friend Agnes is sailing to France, but you shouldn't shut yourself away. Why not make a friend of one of the boys? Henry Edwards is a great lover of animals, and I know you enjoy looking after the rabbits and feeding our pet emu.'

Marion screwed up her face and bit her bottom lip. 'I don't think the boys like me,' she confided, thinking back to how the prefects had ignored her an hour or so ago. Her father often encouraged her to speak to the boys, but she found them mistrustful of her and often unkind. 'They talk to Mama because she gives them treats, but they don't trust *me*. Maybe they think I will tell their secrets to Papa.'

'I doubt you'd do that. You are a perfect angel, Miss Neitenstein.' Mr Leer paused as the footsteps of the boys thundered above them. 'Class seven are coming down here now,' he said with a grimace. Class seven was made up of the worst-behaved boys in the school. 'They're to help me move some of the books for a new display. You better get going or you'll miss the boats to Cockatoo Island. I'll give your mother your books,' he insisted.

## CHAPTER 4

# COCKATOO ISLAND

Arriving on the quarterdeck, Marion blinked as her eyes adjusted to the contrast between the dim library and the glare of the setting sun. She joined the line of boys waiting to row over to the island. Some were looking forward to swimming in the tidal pool, others to a game of cricket.

The boys at the back of the line looked at her once and then shuffled forward, skylarking with one another. So Marion stood awkwardly by herself, arms crossed over her chest, pretending to be interested in her shoes.

The line grew shorter and shorter until those who were left had to cram into the last of the boats. Marion felt left out, standing there in her dress and stockings among a sea of sailor suits.

The prefect organising the seating glanced her way. He was about to leave her on her own but thought better of it. He cocked his head and the boys budged up to make room for her. Marion ignored the mutterings as she sat down.

She was first off the boat when it nudged the jetty on the island, and she headed straight for the animal hutches. Her father, Captain Neitenstein, was watching on as a group of boys used the gymnastic apparatuses. Handsome Mr Mason, the deputy principal, had already headed off with a group of boys for swimming lessons at the pool.

Marion felt that she must at least *try* to get along with the boys, as Mr Leer suggested—and she did love the pets. Normally she spent time with the animals when Agnes visited, or when the boys were busy elsewhere and she had them all to herself.

There were three boys at the hutches when Marion arrived. A fourth boy was following the emu around, scattering seed for her.

'Good evening,' Marion muttered, announcing her presence.

None of the boys shifted from their positions and she was forced to squat behind them, without a good view of the animals. Near her, a boy called Solomon was holding a lop-eared rabbit rather carelessly. The animal whimpered and the boy looked around at her.

Marion smiled sweetly. 'I've read that rabbits like being held close,' she told him.

She hoped he would follow her instructions and ask for further advice. But he just scowled and turned away.

The boy beside him, Henry Edwards, elbowed him, and Solomon said, 'Thanks, Miss.'

Marion knew this was only to save himself from trouble if she decided to tell her father she'd been ignored. Tears were beginning to warm the corners of her eyes. She took a deep breath. 'I read an article by Gordon Stables in the *Boy's Own Paper* yesterday about rabbits,' she told her reluctant audience as brightly as she could, but there was no reply.

Nelson, who was also holding one of the rabbits, stood up abruptly, keen to get away from her.

'May I hold him?' she asked, stepping forward and reaching out for the white rabbit in his hands.

Ignoring her, Nelson returned the animal to its cage. 'If you like,' he said, shrugging. But then he had a sudden change of heart. He snatched the rabbit back out of the hutch and dumped it in her arms. 'Of course, Miss. And thank you for the information,' he said, bowing awkwardly.

It had worked! Marion cuddled the rabbit close to her, beaming at the boys, who continued to watch her. She was wondering which interesting fact she might amaze them with next, when a deep voice behind her interrupted her thoughts.

Marion twisted around. It was her father. Her heart sank. No wonder Nelson was being so polite.

'Lovely to see you all getting along together,' the captain said. Resplendent in his uniform and cap, he towered over the boys and his daughter, his dark eyes surveying them all.

Marion caught Solomon's eyeroll. But Henry Edwards looked apologetically at her. Marion sighed deeply. Her attempt to befriend the boys clearly had *not* worked.

# CHAPTER 5
# A VAGABOND NAMED BRAGG

Marion spent Saturday assisting her mother with errands in town and then chores at home. They rehung the pictures in the parlour, mended three shirts and darned ten pairs of socks and stockings, re-stuffed the piano stool and transferred two indoor ferns into larger pots. They washed and ironed the curtains, and hung them back up. Then they let down the hems of Marion's dresses because she was growing so fast.

Marion was not keen to attend church with the *Sobraon* boys the next day. The last few Sundays had been rainy and the boys had been kept onboard, with religious services conducted in the mess room. This had been a great relief to Marion.

She'd sat quietly, and unseen, at the back of the hall. But this Sunday they were back to the old routine, which involved all but the worst-behaved boys rowing to the Circular Quay. They would then march to church through the streets of Sydney to tunes played by the *Sobraon*'s brass band.

The boys were always on their best behaviour during their Sunday excursions. For some, this was their only experience of Sydney each week, as they were normally allowed on just the ship and Cockatoo Island. They knew that any misbehaviour would earn them a swift demotion into class seven, which was reserved for newcomers and the worst-behaved boys. They were forced to stay behind, washing up and sweeping floors.

Marion trailed along at the back with her mother and Mr Mason, while the ship's brass band and the captain led the parade. Marion and her mother walked in silence, full of their own thoughts.

Mr Mason, on the other hand, was constantly distracted by enthusiastic Sydneysiders rushing up to him.

'How wonderful,' an old woman told him, wiping a tear from her eye and seizing his hand. 'Your boys are a credit to the colony, sir!'

Another passer-by handed Mr Mason a bag of sweets. 'They're prizes, sir, for the orphans.'

But not everyone was pleased to see the marching sailor boys. A group of waifs draped over a fence on Elizabeth Street scattered when they heard the marching band approaching.

One boy remained, however, eager to see if he recognised any of his old friends. His eyes widened. 'George Sumner!' he cried out, waving madly with his hat at one of the *Sobraon* boys.

Sumner looked up, recognised the boy in the ragged clothes, but marched on without acknowledging him. Sumner's old friend pulled his hat over his ears and sloped off down a nearby alleyway, hands in his pockets.

As she marched along, Marion worried away with her big toe at the mend she'd made in her stocking. She hadn't done a very good job of it. She pulled up her stocking to try to resettle the hole, but it pinched her toe, and she had to limp.

These goings-on were observed with interest by a short, brooding man, who had stopped in the gutter to watch.

His name was Joseph Bragg. Bragg's dark, hooded eyes slipped from one *Sobraon* boy to another as they marched past him. He knew many of them.

There was his old protégé Docker, looking well-fed and smart—nothing like the haggard, hungry child Bragg had reared in his den. And there was Carlisle—much taller and stronger now. Bragg spat on the ground. And Freeman and Bowers were there too, smiling at the crowd and looking smart, so different to how he liked them to be. Then Bragg's eyes settled on the tallest man in the parade—the captain of the *Sobraon*. Dutchy. The man who had stolen his boys from him. *Stolen them!*

Bragg sucked in his breath and gritted his teeth. *Dutchy!* There he was, a head and shoulders taller than everyone else, the man who wore away at Bragg's boys the same way the sea breaks up an abandoned ship. Bragg spat again and resumed chewing the wad of tobacco in his mouth. He sneered as the captain moved around the corner.

A stray dog ambled over to Bragg, sniffing hopefully at the ground near the man's feet. Bragg kicked it away, and the dog whimpered and fled.

Bragg pulled his hat low over his face, burrowed his hands deep in his complex coat pockets, and dipped his chin into the stained silk scarf tied around his throat like a noose.

Then he noticed the young girl and her mother at the end of the line of marching boys. The girl limped a little as though something was wrong with her shoes. It was Marion Selina Neitenstein. He saw her often, this girl. *With that limp, she'd be easy to lure away from the group,* he thought. *But not yet—not yet.*

Bragg watched Marion with a satisfied grin on his face. He knew she was missing her friend Mademoiselle Agnes Angelique Celeste Beresford, who had recently sailed for Europe. Miss Agnes had written to Marion just before setting sail. He'd lifted that letter and read all about them.

Spotting the menacing man, Mrs Neitenstein took Marion's hand and steered her closer to the boys. Bragg growled and turned on his heel, intending to head back to his Forty Thieves, who were no doubt sleeping in their den after a busy night. He needed to return to those depths to count the watches, scarfs, rings, necklaces, coins, hats and gloves they had filched for him.

'They're *my* boys,' he growled to himself, casting one last look at the *Sobraon* boys marching away. '*My* little thieves and pickpockets, and I'll do whatever's needed to stop that *Dutchy* taking them from me.'

Bragg moved off effortlessly through the crowd, checking this way and that for easy prey. He stole a lace handkerchief from a lady as she passed by, stuffing it into a pocket deep within his coat. He apologised as he bumped into a gentleman, deftly pocketing the man's gold watch and silver cardcase. As he passed a baker's stall, he grabbed two hot pies without the distracted shopkeeper noticing. Striding up Elizabeth Street in the direction of Surry Hills, Bragg made ground quickly, devouring the pies as he walked, the gravy dribbling down his wrists.

He drew level with Hyde Park, and then span around as a hand grabbed his shoulder. Sliding a knife out of his sleeve, Bragg held it to the throat of the woman who had stopped him. 'This is not the way to win my favour, Mrs Crosscapel,' he hissed, not removing the blade.

The woman's green eyes flicked between the weapon and the man's hooded eyes. She opened her mouth to speak but decided not to. She shifted her shawl around her shoulders and shivered.

Bragg slipped the knife back up his sleeve, but he kept hold of the woman's throat. 'I feel fair trod on by you, Mrs Crosscapel,' he said, wrinkling his nose. 'I provided your family with as much grey as you ask for, and yet you don't feel the need to repay me. I don't enjoy being treated like a fool. I don't appreciate the hullabaloo, see? I've been on the square with you from the start—'

'You've hidden my child from me!' Mrs Crosscapel shrilled, straining to pull away from him. 'I've been searching for him for years. No one but *you* could hide him so well.'

The man smiled thinly as he looked up and down the street, checking to see if the hysterical woman had drawn anyone's attention.

'You kidnapped him,' she insisted. 'Five years he's been missing.'

Bragg pushed her away from him. 'Do I have your boy?' he mused.

Mrs Crosscapel looked at him with hope in her eyes.

He twirled on the spot, sending his coat tails flapping. 'Have I lost sight of him of late, or do I travel to him this very minute? Or did he die of the fever five years ago?' Bragg spat on the ground. 'Perhaps I have indeed taken your boy into the ranks of my street urchins just to teach you a lesson. Perhaps I teach him other lessons too? Am I not kind? How to dive a pocket, sneak budge, be a spieler and nap the regulars. That's how you become a perfect thief, you know.'

Mrs Crosscapel's face dropped.

'Perhaps he chips away at your debt with every trinket he steals,' Bragg sneered. 'Children are blank slates, are they not? Perhaps it is me who writes on your boy now. Tra, la, la!'

## CHAPTER 6

# THE ARRIVAL OF ALEXANDER WALKER

A week passed. Marion slept badly, dreaming about the unkind boys and the pets on Cockatoo Island.

Saturday arrived, and she awoke to the sounds of the boys cleaning the vessel. Officers called out orders to the students checking the rowboats. Whistles blew to direct the boys spidering high up in the rigging looking for fraying ropes. Blasts of cold seawater pummelled the deck above, pumped up from the harbour in thick heavy hoses. There were squeals of delight when the boys splashed each other. They were quickly muffled when the heavy tread of an officer sounded close by.

Before Agnes left, Saturday had been a day of delight for Marion. She would wait for the boys to finish their chores, and then her friend would arrive. Together, they'd read in the library, play on deck or stroll around Cockatoo Island. Marion had been able to bear the boys' sour looks and silences when Agnes was there to distract her.

But now Agnes was hundreds of miles away. Marion pictured her sitting in a tiny cabin with her case open in front of her. She hoped that Agnes would write a letter to her and post it at the next port she visited. Agnes had promised to write often. She even said she'd write a letter while she was still in Sydney, before she set sail, but nothing had arrived. Marion tried not to think about it as she pulled the golden pendant along the chain around her neck.

There was a knock at the door. Her mother entered bearing Marion's favourite cup with a flower-stem handle and blue flowers around the rim. It was Mrs Neitenstein's, and she only took it from its velvet-lined box on special occasions.

'This will help you feel a little better, my dear,' her mother explained. She touched Marion's forehead with the back of her hand. 'No fever, but you're feeling a little down, I think.'

A whistle screeched overhead, and the sound of several sets of sprinting bare feet followed its call. Her mother smiled.

'You will make friends when you go to your new school next year, my dear. And Agnes will become a firm penfriend. But, until then, you and I can be the best of friends—and you have Mr Leer too.'

Marion smiled. 'Thank you, Mama. I'm not so sad. I have plenty to read and I've been doing all the puzzles I can find.'

Her mother kissed her on the top of her head. 'Good. Now, get dressed and come out when you're ready to eat.'

A few minutes later, Marion entered her family's private parlour with a newspaper under her arm. She was carefully carrying the special cup, which was now empty. As she settled down in her seat at the table, her mother set a boiled egg in a pretty yellow eggcup in front of her.

Once Marion had finished eating, her mother began braiding her hair. 'What's in the newspaper, my dear?' she asked as she laid out a ribbon flat on the table and then separated Marion's hair into strands.

'It's from last weekend, Mama,' Marion replied. 'I've read all the articles and notices. Now I'm up to the classifieds.'

'The *classifieds*?' laughed her mother. 'Not the most interesting of reading!'

'Some of them are, Mama,' Marion replied. 'Listen to this.' And she turned to the back sheets of the newspaper and read:

Holloway's pills and ointment.—Catarrh Cured.—The number of cases beginning with common cold, ending in incurable chest disease, are positively appalling. Holloway's Pills, assisted by friction with his Ointment on throat and chest, will prevent all danger.

MISSING FRIENDS.

If Joseph Griffiths, who used to work with William Willcock as a shipwright at Port Nicholson, Wellington, New Zealand, about 40 years ago, will communicate with the undersigned he will hear something to his advantage. If he is dead and has left children living they should apply.

W. H. Quick, Solicitor,

Wellington, New Zealand.

The call of the bugle sounded again before Marion could finish. Her mother tied the ribbon on the end of her plait and tapped her shoulder. 'Up you get. Let's go and watch your father dismiss the boys for the weekend.'

Marion's shoulders drooped, but her mother took her hand and pulled her out the parlour door. They arrived on the quarterdeck and took their places behind the captain and his officers.

It was early December, the morning was warm and Marion wished she'd brought her hat. She shielded her eyes from the sun and gazed over the ranks of boys before her. The staff's uniforms were perfect, their brass buttons and patent leather shoes gleaming. And the boys looked very smart standing to attention in their white sailor suits.

Marion shuffled beside her mother as the captain and Mr Mason descended the steps and walked along the rows of boys, occasionally asking questions, and receiving brief but polite replies. She watched her father's hat with its black peak move through the mass of boys. Once or twice the captain asked Mr Mason to make a note. One boy's trousers flapped about his calves and he obviously needed a new uniform. Another boy's fringe was in his eyes and he needed to see the barber.

Otherwise, all was quiet, except for the woosh of a swooping gull and the distant calls of ferry staff. Everybody swayed slightly as the ship moved on the gentle swell. Every eye followed the captain. When he approached, the boys braced themselves, like people do for a lightning strike during a storm. There was a collective sigh of relief as the captain returned to the raised platform of the quarterdeck.

'Morning, boys.' Captain Neitenstein's voice boomed out across the deck at the boys mustered below him. It was as loud as the crash of waves against rocks. 'You've worked well this week, and I was especially impressed with the efficiency of your cleaning this morning. The ship is a credit to you, and you are a credit to it.'

He paused to allow a cheer from the school. He raised his hand, and the cheer died instantly. 'Our band is booked this afternoon to play at the Botanic Gardens. Band boys, meet Mr Bourke on deck at two o'clock. The prefects will row you over in plenty of time. Mr Mason will be conducting swimming lessons at our pool this afternoon. If you're in classes three or four, meet him there *punctually* at three o'clock.'

Captain Neitenstein paused and frowned at the assembled boys. 'Punishments,' he said briskly, consulting a black notebook in his hand.

The cohort of boys watched intently. Marion's stomach lurched. It was the feeling she had when she waded out into the surf and could no longer touch the seafloor with her toes.

'None! There are no demotions this week,' the captain announced.

Both Marion and the boys relaxed as if they had found shallow water.

'Promotions,' he went on, more brightly.

Marion's attention was caught by the boys from class seven at the front of the assembly. They slouched around, their eyes following the staff, waiting for an opportunity to mutter to each other. Two staff stood close by, ready to jump on poor behaviour, but they couldn't see the boys' faces.

A large boy called Norman Roth rolled his eyes as an officer passed by. Marion had been aware of Roth since he'd arrived on board over a year ago. The captain called him 'incorrigible', the naughtiest boy in class seven. Normally boys remained in that class for a week or two, but Roth had been a member since his arrival.

On his first day on the *Sobraon* he had refused to eat and had even thrown his bread overboard. He'd been caned four times during a muster, with the stick the captain carried at all times. Then a few months ago Roth had been flogged for the theft of another boy's comb. And Marion had only seen Roth pick up a book once. He'd read the first page, mouthing the words, and then shoved it back on the shelf, upside down.

A gull landed on the railing nearby as the captain read out the names of those being promoted. 'Henry Holland and Angus Waterford!' he boomed, frightening the gull and Marion. 'Promotion from class seven to class six for diligent completion of work.' There was a round of applause. 'Simon Lang, Christopher Sanderson and Peter Walsh, promotion from class five to class four for hard work this week clearing the recreation ground.' A short cheer went up. 'And congratulations to George Sumner for his apprenticeship to a farmer in Singleton.'

There was more cheering, followed by an expectant hush.

Everyone was eagerly awaiting the captain's next announcement. George was in the first class and would need replacing when he left for the countryside. Promotion to that class was coveted by every boy in the second class.

'He will be replaced by William Salt,' the captain announced.

The ship was rocked by cheering, and William Salt was surrounded by boys whistling and shouting and punching the air. Behind him, Norman Roth was being told off by a red-faced officer for making a rude gesture.

The captain looked to Mr Mason. 'All right, Mr Mate?' he asked.

Mr Mason nodded in a soldier-like fashion, withdrew a silver whistle from his breast pocket and blew a clear signal. '*Sobraon* boys, man the yards!' he cried.

The boys from classes one to six sprang into action, clambering up the masts and along the yards. Each pupil knew his position, with some climbing all the way to the top of the masts. Once there, standing with their feet carefully placed along the yards, they balanced themselves by placing one hand on their neighbour's shoulder.

The staff, Marion and Mrs Neitenstein applauded as they

craned their necks to get a view of the magnificent spectacle above them. Mr Mason blew the whistle again and the boys reversed their monkeying and returned to the deck.

The band struck up a tune and the boys marched to their places of recreation, for the work was over. Some marched down to the library, others to the mess room for craft activities. The remainder formed neat groups on the deck as they waited for the boats to take them to Cockatoo Island. Norman Roth and class seven were escorted below decks to clean the cutlery.

In this organised chaos, Marion moved away from her mother, who was speaking with William Salt about sewing an anchor badge onto his uniform to mark him out as a prefect. Marion moved along the deck and looked over the rails. A group of boys already lined the gangway, pushing each other aside to get to the rowboats first.

At that moment, a jolly boat came alongside. The jostling boys moved aside as a policeman arrived on deck, bringing with him a tall, blonde-haired boy. He had dirty smudges on the front of his shirt and a livid bruise on his temple.

Marion recognised him as the rough who had attacked the tradesman near the Loong Shan Tea House over a week ago. Several of the boys nearby stopped what they were doing and elbowed each other. One or two nodded at the boy, but he didn't acknowledge them. Instead, he closely watched the captain, who was beside him and the policeman in an instant.

'Look at me, lad,' Captain Neitenstein demanded. The boy defied the order. He flinched as the captain forced his head up by pushing his cane under his chin. The boy scowled up at the captain.

'His name's Alexander Walker, sir,' the policeman said.

The boys moving down the gangway strained to get a good look at the new boy.

'Thinks himself pretty hard, I'd say,' the policeman continued. 'Been in the Forty Thieves push, see. But I heard him crying in his cell last night.' The policeman chuckled unkindly.

Marion stared at the new boy. He was thin but strong-looking, and his clothes were too big for him. Now that she was closer, she could see the bruises and sores on his legs and face. And she wasn't surprised when he scratched his head with a vigour that indicated lice. This was not unusual in new *Sobraon* boys.

Marion thought of her soft bed, wardrobe full of clothes, hot breakfasts, and trips to places like the Loong Shan Tea House. Alexander Walker had never enjoyed such things. She wondered where he usually slept at night. She might have felt sorry for him, but there was something about the way he stared up at her father that made her shiver.

Like most of the boys on the ship, Marion was scared of Norman Roth, but there was something even more threatening about Walker. Roth could barely string a sentence together, but intelligence sparkled in this boy's eyes.

'Perhaps he was crying because no one has ever looked after him,' the captain suggested, eyeing Walker closely and speaking more to him than the policeman.

*Why on earth does Papa always think the best of these boys?* Marion wondered. *He even believes Norman Roth will one day get an apprenticeship, but I doubt that will ever happen.*

'The coppers thrashed me, sir!' Walker blurted out. 'An' I never had no mother or nothin' to feed me. I had to swipe things to eat, and the Forty Thieves—'

'That's enough, you larrikin,' the policeman interrupted, rolling his eyes and shaking his head.

'An' this six foot of tripe said all kinds on the way over here, lickin' me into shape an' threatenin' to make me warm if I don't co-operate with you.'

'No police officer has laid a hand on you. You were arrested a week ago and the judge sent you here, fair and square.' Walker tried to interrupt, but the policeman ploughed on. 'You should use this as an opportunity to change your life—get an honest calling. The staff here'll teach you your lessons and get you a job. Better'n being in and out of gaol for the rest of your life.'

Walker spat on the deck, clenched his fists and screamed, 'Shut your garret, you lump o' jaw! I've taken bigger than you in the street.'

The captain grabbed Walker's arm, anger forking across his face like lightning. His fingers locked around the boy's scrawny wrist and he flicked his cane at the boy's hand. The *thwack* echoed across the deck.

The boys waiting in line cringed and averted their eyes.

'I will not tolerate such language on this ship, Walker!'

the captain thundered, his piercing eyes wide and terrifying. Walker shrank a little and cradled his hand to his chest, whimpering. The other boys watched on, fascinated.

Glancing between Walker and the captain, the policeman lifted his hat. 'Good luck with this one, Captain. We've been trying for a long time to get 'im, and here he finally is. I'll see myself off.' He pushed past the boys and dashed down the gangway.

'Wasn't the copper's smarts as got me—those gigglemugged turncoats fled 'n' left me alone to go in the prison van,' Walker mumbled.

Captain Neitenstein said nothing. He wasn't surprised that Walker had been let down by his crew. The captain considered him from his great height, peering at him through bushy eyebrows. Then he steered Walker to the railing to look out over the water. He paused, in the same way the wind does before a strong gust hits. 'See that?' the captain asked, pointing with his cane. 'Deepest water in the harbour. This ship is inescapable. The last boy who tried drowned. Understand?'

Walker nodded. There was a pause, and he added, 'Yes, *sir*.'

Neitenstein ignored the hint of sarcasm in the boy's voice. He turned on his heel and pointed at a large sign bolted to one of the ship's masts.

'Can you read?' he asked.

'Yes, sir. And write. But I can't remember who taught me. It wasn't the man I've been shiftin' with—'

The captain was not listening. 'Read and understand *that*,' he ordered.

Walker looked up and squinted. The large plaque read:

> THIS TABLE SHOWS THE CONDUCT OF EVERY BOY ON BOARD. BOYS, WHEN COMING ON THE VESSEL, ARE PLACED IN NO. VII CLASS, FROM WHICH THEY CAN RISE BY OBTAINING GOOD MARKS FROM THEIR OFFICERS. A CERTAIN NUMBER OF MARKS GAINED BY INDUSTRY WILL RAISE ANY BOY IN RANK IN THE INSTITUTION. BAD CONDUCT AND IDLENESS WILL CAUSE HIM TO BE REDUCED AND DEPRIVE HIM OF THE

PRIVILEGES HE HAS EARNED; WITH THE POWER, HOWEVER, OF RE-EARNING GOOD MARKS AND REGAINING HIS POSITION BY SUBSEQUENT GOOD CONDUCT. EACH BOY MUST BEAR IN MIND THAT THE MANY PRIVILEGES OF THE SHIP, WHICH ARE ACCESSIBLE TO ALL ON BOARD, ARE EARNED BY SIMPLY BEHAVING IN A PROPER MANNER, AND SO GAINING THE RESPECT OF THE OFFICERS.

'You'll be in class seven to start with,' the captain informed Walker. 'But with good behaviour and a respectful attitude you should rise up the ranks quickly. I expect it of you, just as I do of every boy here. Mr Mason will take you to the barber for a haircut and provide you with a uniform. Welcome to the Nautical School Ship *Sobraon*.'

## CHAPTER 7

# LIGHT FINGERS

'It's nice to see you out and about again, Miss,' Henry Edwards said quietly.

It was a sunny January afternoon a few weeks later and Cockatoo Island was swarming with boys making the most of the sun and the sea breeze. The emu pecked around a large group of boys playing cricket. Every now and then a cry went up as someone caught the ball or hit a six. On the far side of the island, boys splashed around in the swimming pool.

Marion sat alone in the shade of the rabbit hutches, the *Sobraon* moored before her. She jumped at Henry's voice, and gripped the rabbit she was holding in her arms. She squinted up at Henry from under the wide brim of her hat.

'I thought you must be ill,' Henry said. 'We've not seen you out here for a month, nor Miss Beresford neither. And, last time you were here, Solomon was horrible to you. I didn't say anything then, but I should've. I'm sorry.'

'I've been busy helping mother, and Agnes has sailed for France,' Marion replied. She hadn't really been busy. She'd spent Christmas cooped up in her room, and she'd only ventured out today because her mother was angry with her for being so sad because she hadn't received any letters from Agnes.

When she'd stepped onto the island, Marion had been relieved to see the boys busy with their games. She'd settled down to pet the rabbits and be miserable on her own. Her mother couldn't punish her for that.

'Well, I'm pleased to see you, Miss, and to see you so well,' Henry said, twisting his cap in his hands. His sailor suit was well looked after—he'd even darned a small hole in one of the sleeves himself.

'Why don't you play cricket with the others?' Marion asked.

Henry pointed to his left eye. 'I can't see out of this eye, Miss. Makes games dangerous. And I prefer the animals anyway.

I hope the captain sends me to the countryside when my time comes.'

He beamed as he shuffled to one side, and Marion noticed for the first time that he also had a limp.

'Did you have an accident?' she asked, moving to make room for him near the hutches. As he reached up to choose an animal to hold, she noticed that he used his right arm, not his left.

'Born like this, I think.' Henry shrugged as he settled back down on the grass. 'Pa deserted Ma when I was born. Said he was going to the goldfields to make his fortune, but he never came back. Ma said he was ashamed of me and that was the real reason he didn't return.' Henry looked sadly at his left arm.

'She told you that?'

Jumbo the dog bounded over, his tail thrashing excitedly as he settled down beside Henry. Henry fondled Jumbo's soft ears and nodded. 'Ma had a hard life while she was alive. She was a washerwoman, and her hands were always sore and blistered from the hot water.' He swallowed. 'One day, she just didn't come home. I looked and looked for her, but nothing.'

He stroked the rabbit on his lap and smiled as it nibbled

his fingers. Marion noticed that Henry's eyes were swollen, as though he'd been crying.

'I'd never been to school, so I just went around with some boys I met. We used to steal things. We burgled a house once. I wasn't very good at it 'cause of my arm. An' then I was caught and came here. It was a relief, to be honest. Everyone says this place is a terror, but that's only if you're bad.'

Marion thought of Norman Roth being flogged in front of the ship's company. By the end of it, he had marks on his back like the deep scratches a cat's claws make. She shivered.

Henry and Marion sat quietly, gazing around the island. The emu was flapping her stubby wings at the boys beside the fence. The cricket game was at change-over time, and a new group was taking the field. A bag of lollies was the prize for the winners, and the boys were casting hungry glances at the brown-paper packet, which Mr Mason had placed on a stool nearby.

Out on the harbour, beyond the *Sobraon*, steamers and ferries putted by. A pleasure cruiser zipped past, a band playing on the deck to a group of glamourous ladies and gentlemen sitting in wicker chairs and drinking from tall glasses. Beyond them, a man-o-war was being pulled into position by a tugboat.

'Mr Leer taught me to read,' Henry continued. 'I never thought I'd be able to do that. It's much better being here than out on the streets with the Forty Thieves.'

Marion almost dropped the rabbit. '*You* were in the Forty Thieves?'

'Yeah. Quite a few of the boys here were part of that push.' He pointed them out with his good hand. 'Docker and Carlisle over there talking to Mr Mason. Freeman and Bowers. And Walker, of course.'

Alexander Walker had been promoted to class six just before Christmas. He was now playing cricket with his friends. The boy at the wicket eyed Walker as he bowled. The ball was released, spinning rapidly, and the wicket exploded. A cheer went up and several boys rushed forward to hoist Walker onto their shoulders.

'Walker is popular wherever he goes,' Henry said quietly. 'He was a great favourite of—' Henry swallowed and whispered the name, 'Mr Bragg.'

Another boy took over the role of bowler, and Walker found a position on the field without a word. The batter hit the next ball high over the heads of the spectators and it landed with a thump on the side of one of the rabbit hutches.

Shocked by the noise, the rabbit in Marion's arms convulsed, and Jumbo let out a short, sharp bark. The trembling rabbit scurried up Marion's shoulder and nestled its head in her neck before trying to escape down her back.

Walker, who was chasing after the ball, appeared behind Marion. He tried to retrieve the animal before it escaped, but his hand and the rabbit's paws got tangled in her necklace.

'Sorry, Miss, here you go,' he said, handing the rabbit safely back to her. He picked up the ball and lobbed it back to the bowler. Turning to Henry, he asked quietly, 'You fine now, Edwards?'

Marion looked to Henry for an explanation. 'Norman Roth tripped me up on deck and laughed at me, so Walker sorted him out.'

'I should've taken off my coat proper,' Walker said, a terrible look on his face. 'I had enough of that Roth in the push—'

'Roth was in the Forty Thieves *too*?' Marion asked.

Walker looked amused as he ran his hand through his hair. 'Heaps of us were. He was a brute out there,' he waved his hand in the direction of the Circular Quay, 'just as he is here. He's pretty thick, too.'

'And why were *you* in the Forty Thieves,' Marion asked, 'with that horrible man, Bragg?'

Henry went pale but Walker's eyes sparkled.

'Bragg ain't so scary. He's tough an' won't suffer fools, but he brought me up when my parents didn't.'

'He's cruel and wicked, Walker,' Henry cut in, darkly. 'He'd do any one of his boys in if they put a step wrong. What do you think happens to them boys who don't come back? Think they're out in the country ridin' ponies? Dead in some ditch, more like.'

Walker screwed up his face. 'He don't like idlers, that's for sure. And I'm always keen to follow his orders.' Walker shifted his feet. 'But he fed me and protected me when my ma and pa were dead. And that's worth something. He appreciates honour.'

Henry snorted and Walker looked annoyed.

'I *say*, boys,' a man interrupted in a posh voice, 'I've just come from the ferry, and I'd appreciate a hand getting to the *Sobraon*.'

The gentleman who spoke was pink-cheeked and sweaty in

his dark woollen suit. He wore a jewelled pin in his cravat and a gold ring on his pinkie finger. A folio of papers and a newspaper were tucked under one arm.

'Certainly, sir,' Walker said politely.

Marion raised her eyebrows as Walker saluted the visitor. Walker had been positively vicious when he arrived, but these days he was acting like a model student.

'Excellent, excellent,' the man said. 'I have an appointment with your captain in twenty minutes.'

'I'd be happy to row you over to the ship, sir,' Walker said.

Marion stood up and deposited her rabbit gently back in its hutch. 'Hello, Mr Inglis,' she said, adjusting her hat.

'Miss Neitenstein!' the Minister for Education cried. 'How wonderful to see you looking so well, out here in the sunshine.' He waved the folio of papers over his face, seeking a breeze. Then he whispered, so Walker and Henry couldn't hear, 'If only my business with your father was as pleasant.' He indicated the newspaper in his hand.

Walker leaned forward, straining to hear what the minister was saying.

Marion ignored him. *What on earth does Mr Inglis mean?*

she wondered. *He's always praising Papa. In fact, everyone says how wonderful the ship is, including the Colonial Secretary and Mr Tart.*

Henry excused himself, and he and Jumbo hurried off to see to the emu, which was still pecking around the perimeter fence.

Walker set off to make the jolly boat ready, and in no time at all Mr Inglis, Marion and Walker were in the boat, with Walker pulling hard on the oars as they sliced through the water towards the *Sobraon*.

As they neared the ship, Marion heard the staff instructing the boys in class seven, who were still on board completing their chores. She wondered why there seemed to be more boys there than usual.

Mr Inglis had his eyes closed and his lips pressed firmly together in a painful grimace. His papers were at his feet.

'Are you seasick, Mr Inglis?' Marion asked. He nodded, gripping the side of the boat.

Walker rowed on in silence, staring out at the harbour.

Marion glanced at Mr Inglis. His eyes were still closed, so she reached over and grabbed his newspaper. She gasped as she read the headline: 'N.S.S. *Sobraon* a failure: Boys returning to the ship, sent back for bad behaviour from apprenticeships; Captain Neitenstein to lose his job due to boys' rioting.' The article carried a photo of her father in a particularly angry-looking pose.

Marion glanced up at the large number of class-seven boys on deck and blushed. Her father would be angry at them for misbehaving so badly that they'd been brought back to the ship. She quickly replaced the newspaper.

Walker brought the jolly boat alongside. The mammoth bulk of the *Sobraon* creaked beside them, and Marion felt very small indeed. Straddling the boat and the gangway, Walker helped Mr Inglis onto the platform, and then, to her surprise, did the same for Marion.

Mr Inglis plucked a silver coin from his breast pocket. 'Thank you, young master,' he said, passing Walker the coin. Walker's eyes widened and he slipped the money into his pocket, thanking the minister with another salute.

Mr Inglis mounted the stairs, but Marion turned back and

called out to Walker. He had shown her kindness by helping her out of the boat, so she thought she'd return the favour. 'Boys normally add that kind of money into a common pool.' His face was blank, so she added, 'It's for prizes and things like that.'

Walker shrugged and stared at her, as if daring her to make a fuss. Then he patted his pocket and turned away.

Marion frowned. She knew if the other boys found out, they wouldn't be happy. But she had no choice but to hurry after the minister and then show him to her father's office, where he was speedily admitted. The door slammed shut behind him.

Marion peered down the corridor. Seeing no one, she removed her hat and put her ear to the thick mahogany door.

'It's simply unacceptable,' she heard Mr Inglis say, as a fist slammed onto a wooden desk.

The captain's voice rumbled in response. Marion pressed her ear harder to the door.

'Be that as it may, Captain, the press is writing this up and the stories are not a credit to this institution. Look at this!' he said. Marion heard the rustling of the newspaper. '*Sobraon* boys apprenticed up on the Manning River,' Inglis read, 'have this week run riot throughout the neighbourhood. One boy was caught stealing a horse and another three silver candlesticks from a local resident. Another boy set fire to his master's barn, and a fourth absconded and was found by the police hiding in bushland. All the boys have been returned to the *Sobraon*, where the general public might reasonably hope that the captain will make some effort to curb their behaviour.' Inglis paused. 'Well, Neitenstein, what do you say to that?'

Chair legs scraped on the floor as the captain stood up. 'It is true, Minister,' he said, 'that we have had a rather large number of boys returned—boys I have *ordered* back to the ship, mind you. But some of those boys are hard eggs, members of the local gangs—'

'The Forty Thieves? The King Mob?'

'Of course. And they take *time* to train.'

'You've never had anything like this happen before?'

'No.'

'And do you have a sense of *why* they are suddenly failing at their apprenticeships? Or an understanding of why a large number of boys suddenly decided to go against their training and attack their masters?'

'No!' the captain declared.

'And what would you have me say when I am questioned about this in parliament?'

'Tell them that I will not lionise these boys. They are in class seven again with no recreational activities, just chores. Sometimes brutal boys need brutal treatment to change them. I am dealing with it.'

Mr Inglis said nothing.

'And is my job in peril, as it says here?' asked the captain in a strained voice.

Again, Marion heard the newspaper rustling.

'Your situation is precarious, sir,' Mr Inglis declared.

## CHAPTER 8
# THROUGH THE PORTHOLE

Marion's golden pendant was missing. She felt foolish for losing it—she was sure Agnes would still have hers. As she sat at the dinner table in her family's private apartment on the ship that evening, Marion was too embarrassed to mention it.

Her father was in a foul mood after his meeting with the minister. He hacked into his roast lamb as if he were slaughtering the animal all over again. Her mother, who sat at the opposite end of the table, was not feeling well and was pushing a few peas and slices of carrot around her plate with her fork.

Marion chewed her meat, bowing her head to avoid attention. She stared at the white tablecloth. *When I grow up, I'll have colourful patterned tablecloths that don't stain easily,* Marion thought as she shifted her napkin to hide the spatters of gravy.

Her father finished his meal in record-fast time, laid down his cutlery and pushed his plate forward with a 'Harumph!'

Marion and her mother exchanged worried glances.

'My dear,' Mrs Neitenstein began, sympathy in her eyes, 'this will all be sorted out in the shortest time. The boys who have come back will be re-trained by your officers and returned to their masters to begin their apprenticeships again. The newspapers have their sensational stories now, but soon they will be forced to report how your men have won the day and reminded those boys how to behave. All will be well again very soon.'

The captain took a moment to speak. The frosted-glass lamp above his head flickered as it swung from the ceiling.

'Thank you, my dears,' he said, smiling sadly at both his wife and daughter. 'I've never been in a situation like this. It is *terribly* rare for a boy to fail at his apprenticeship. I bring very few of them back to the ship for bad behaviour. And now I have ten returned in one week!'

'Henry Edwards says that most of them are from the same

gang—' Marion began, but her father spoke over her.

'Mr Mason cannot make head nor tail of it either. We are all baffled.' The captain shook his head and crossed his arms over his belly. The brass buttons on his coat and the grey hairs in his beard glistened in the lantern light.

Marion squeezed his hand.

'At least I have you under control, little one,' he told her, patting her shoulder. 'Are you looking forward to starting at your new school soon? Your mother says the Latin master there is excellent.'

'Yes, Mr Leer was telling me about him,' Marion said.

Her father's face clouded again and he tapped a finger on his cheek. He fished a crinkled piece of yellowish paper from his pocket. 'I nearly forgot. Mr Leer handed this to me, but he couldn't make it out. The boys were passing it around in class. Mr Leer confiscated it when none of them would explain what it meant. It's gibberish to me.' He was about to hand her the paper when there was a knock at the door.

'The guests are arriving, sir,' Mr Mason called through the door.

Her father folded up the note and shoved it back in his pocket. 'The Lantern Talk starts in twenty minutes, Marion,' he reminded her as he stood up. 'Tidy yourself up and then come down and join us. What's the topic tonight, Mason?' he asked, as he opened the door.

'Life in China, sir.'

'Capital, capital.'

As soon as her parents and Mr Mason were gone, Marion leapt up. She'd already decided to use the time to retrace her steps and find her pendant. She would check her room first, and then move to the corridor near her father's office where she'd knelt to listen through the door.

As Marion stepped out of the dining room into the corridor, her eye was caught by a piece of paper on the floor. She picked it up. It had a yellow stain on it, and she realised that it must have fallen out of her father's pocket. She unfolded it and immediately saw why neither her father nor Mr Leer could understand it. It was written in code.

Marion looked around. She could hear the boys assembling in the schoolroom below. As tonight was a special occasion, the ship was illuminated, and through a nearby porthole she saw the glow of fairy lights on the masts of the ship reflected in the dark, deep water. She shifted towards the light and angled the paper to get a better look at it. Her hand went to her throat as it always did when she was thinking, but it found no necklace to fiddle with. Marion's stomach lurched as she peered at the paper. Twelve individual ink smears, arranged in two lines, covered the page.

There were footsteps in the corridor and Marion flattened the paper against her chest.

'Miss Neitenstein,' Mr Leer called out over the pile of books in his arms, 'I trust you're going to the Lantern Talk?'

'Yes, in a minute, Mr Leer.'

'Lovely. See you there. I'll just put these books back in the library for the boys to reshelve later and I'll be there too.'

'Hang on, Mr Leer!' Marion cried, as she stuffed the note into her belt. She searched the towering pile of books in his arms. 'May I?' she asked, gesturing to one of the books. 'I think this is the one.'

'Of course—a little less weight for me,' Mr Leer replied, heaving the pile of books higher. 'Now, run back and leave that book in your room, or you'll be late for the talk.'

Marion rushed to her room, lit a lantern and flipped quickly through the book. Next to her, spread out on her quilt, was the cryptic note. Her eyes scanned heading after heading—'How I Became a Conjurer', 'Queen of the Serpents', 'A Coral Prison'. And then she found it, 'More Ink Blurs'.

Marion's hands shook as she scanned the article about how to write secret messages by blurring ink. She compared the illustrations in the book to the note beside her, found a pen and another scrap of paper, and recorded her translation. Her eyes widened. In the mess of ink was a clear message, 'TONIGHT ALEX W'.

*Is that Alexander Walker?* she wondered.

There was a *clunk* outside the porthole beside her. Marion yanked open the lace curtain and peered out. But all she could see was her own reflection—a weary girl with a thin, pale face and a dark plait resting over one shoulder. Marion extinguished the light in her room and returned to the window. It took her eyes a few moments to adjust, and at first she wasn't sure what she was seeing. She squinted, and things became clearer.

A rowboat bobbed beside the *Sobraon*. The man in it was pulling something heavy out of the water. Marion gasped. It was one of the boys—she could see his white sailor suit in the gloom. Was it Alexander Walker? The boy was wrestled from the water onto the boat, where he sat hunched in the stern as the man rowed with all his might away from the ship, heading east towards the Circular Quay.

Marion folded up the note, slid it into the large book and placed it on the shelf at the foot of her bed. She swapped her velvet jacket for a duck-egg blue cape and tied a white and sea-green striped ribbon onto the end of her plait. She dusted her shoes with her handkerchief and left the room.

# CHAPTER 9
# THE MAGIC LANTERN

By the time Marion arrived on deck, only a few guests were milling around and the rowboat was nowhere to be seen. No one else appeared to have noticed anything odd.

Mr Mason was on the quarterdeck, herding guests into the schoolroom below. 'Miss Neitenstein, this is Mrs Crosscapel,' he said, gesturing to the pretty, dark-haired lady by his side. 'She has an interest in the ship and is keen to see tonight's presentation. Could you take her down to the schoolroom and find her a seat?'

Mrs Crosscapel was tall and slender, with hollow cheeks and bright eyes. She wore an old grey skirt and clutched a black shawl around her shoulders. Her shoes were polished but were worn down at the heels. She dressed like someone who had fallen on hard times and was now making-do.

'I'm the captain's daughter,' Marion explained as she led Mrs Crosscapel down the stairs.

Mrs Crosscapel's eyes widened in delight. 'You would know *all* the boys here then, my dear. Are there any named Crosscapel?' And then she added, a little harshly, 'Think carefully. *Please.*'

Marion shook her head. 'I'm sure such a surname would stick in my mind.'

Mrs Crosscapel looked crestfallen. 'Will *all* the boys be present tonight?' she asked.

Marion had the distinct impression she was being interrogated, but she politely answered the lady's question. 'Most of them—although those in the lowest class are not allowed to be here. And some of the shyer boys prefer to read on nights like this.' Marion thought of Henry Edwards, who she was sure would be in the library practising his letters, with Jumbo by his side.

She pushed open the door to the classroom. The space had been opened up to fit the entire school population, and it was lit with fairy lights around the walls. The boys sat cross-legged on the floor, with the staff and adult visitors ranged around them on chairs. Everyone faced a large white wall made of plaster of Paris, which was ready to receive the slide projections from a handsome magic lantern. The lantern was a large mahogany box with two brass funnels protruding from its front. Slides were inserted into the box to project pictures onto the wall.

Marion found Mrs Crosscapel a seat at the side of the room and sat down beside her. They had to strain their necks to look at the screen, but Marion found the position useful for scanning the boys' faces in search of Walker.

Captain Neitenstein moved to the front of the room, and the boys quietened immediately. 'Good evening boys, staff and guests!' he boomed, hooking his thumbs into the pockets of his waistcoat.

Marion looked along the first and then the second row, examining face after face.

'Tonight we have a very interesting speaker who is going to tell us about his homeland, China,' the captain continued. 'Please welcome Mr Quong Tart.'

There was a hearty round of applause from the boys. They knew that wherever Mr Tart went there naturally followed a feast of cakes, sweets and scones.

Mr Tart rose from his seat and bowed deeply. 'It is my pleasure to be here tonight, teachers, boys, and other guests. I never pass up an opportunity to provide for the most deserving in the colony—and this is such a fine institution.'

*Mr Inglis might disagree with that*, thought Marion.

'I will speak a little about my homeland, and then, with the captain's permission, we will retire to the mess room for a special supper.'

The boys cheered again, and Marion continued scanning the faces before her. Mrs Crosscapel was doing the same.

Mr Tart began his presentation with slides depicting his homeland. The first photograph showed a busy city.

'Like one or two of you boys, I was born in the Canton district in China,' he began, his face open, a friendly look in his eyes. 'But as a boy I was intrigued by the West—the countries in the "centre of the earth", as my father put it. My parents tried to talk me out of travelling. They did not want me to have adventures. My father had run his own business for many years. He wanted me to live my life in his shop, in the district where I grew up. But I did not want to spend my days dusting ornaments and selling knick-knacks.'

Mr Tart paused for a moment.

'I bet many of the boys here would agree with that,' Marion whispered to Mrs Crosscapel. 'At least they can go on apprenticeships. I wish I could go somewhere interesting too!' Mrs Crosscapel ignored her.

Mr Tart continued. 'Did you know that there's a belief in China that Westerners are red-headed man-eaters? But I was still determined to come here!'

There was a rumble of laughter from the audience, and Marion noticed that Mrs Crosscapel was barely listening, her body rigid as she stared out at the mass of sailor suits before her.

A new slide clicked onto the screen. It showed a huge ship sitting at an unfamiliar port. The changeover of slides illuminated the faces of some of the boys sitting in partial darkness. None of them was Alexander Walker.

Quong Tart went on, 'If adventures will not befall a young man in his own village, he must seek them abroad. When I was nine, I convinced my uncle to take me with him from China to the Australian goldfields. We journeyed for a long time, and when we arrived I was stunned by the sights to be seen! I rode my pony up and down the goldfields with one of the mine owners, acting as translator for those who could not speak English.'

Mr Tart mimed riding a pony this way and that, bending down with a hand cupped to his ear. Then he bid goodbye to his imaginary pony, much to the amusement of some of the younger boys, who were watching him with wide eyes and open mouths.

'I blush to say this—you will think me very silly—but as I rode around the fields I was astounded that the gold was not sitting about in great lumps on the surface. I thought my life would be all gold and no work, but instead it was all work and very little gold! Though I am a hard worker, I realised that life on the goldfields was not for me. So I came to Sydney and opened a shop selling silks and teas imported from my home country. And then I opened my famous tearooms!'

As she listened, Marion continued to search the room for Alexander Walker, but he was not there. She was sure of it.

Mr Tart completed his presentation and there was another round of applause, followed by questions from the audience. At a signal from Mr Mason, a few of the boys in the back row stood up and marched out of the room. Separating herself from Mrs Crosscapel, whose attention had been on the boys and not Mr Tart, Marion hurried to join them.

'We are setting up for supper,' Mr Mason told her. 'We would be glad of your help.'

Marion nodded. 'I'll return to collect Mrs Crosscapel once Mr Tart has finished answering questions. Are all the boys in the lecture room tonight, Mr Mason?' she whispered as they moved out into the corridor and headed for the mess room.

'Yes, except for Edwards, who is working in the library, and the boys in class seven, who are on Cockatoo Island, sweeping the wharf area.' Mr Mason stopped and looked at her. 'Why do you ask? Is someone missing?'

'No, not at all. I just wondered.'

In the mess room, the boys began breaking open the crates of cakes, sweets and scones and setting them out on the tables. They made it clear they didn't want help from Marion, so she hovered on the edge of the room straightening the dishes and feeling useless.

As Mr Mason began his tour of the room, checking their work, and the boys stood back to have their arrangements praised, Marion slipped out. She almost tripped over Mrs Crosscapel in the hall. The lady had her hand on a doorknob as she peered into one of the offices.

'Oh! You startled me, dear,' Mrs Crosscapel declared, gathering her shawl about her and clutching at her throat. She smoothed down her shawl distractedly.

'What are you doing here, Mrs Crosscapel?' Marion asked as politely as possible. 'You've wandered a long way from the schoolroom.'

'It's such an interesting institution, my dear, I just wanted to see a bit more of it. A guided tour perhaps?'

'We are more than happy to show you around, madam,' Mr Mason interjected, popping his head around the mess room door. 'You may inquire of the captain on Mondays and Thursdays, and I will be more than happy to assist. For the time being though, perhaps you might care for a cup of Mr Tart's delicious brew and a scone?'

Taking a final glance around her, Mrs Crosscapel reluctantly followed Mr Mason into the hall.

Soon the mess room was packed with people feasting on Mr Tart's treats. Marion drank the cup of tea handed to her by her mother and ate a glazed fruit tart, but she barely tasted either. And she hardly noticed the ices, the Swiss meringues, the rhubarb pies or the slices of sponge cake. All she could think about was Walker and how he had escaped from the ship.

Across the room, Mr Mason was pointing out the features of the hall to Mrs Crosscapel. Nearby, Marion's father had put on a jovial face, obviously trying to forget his meeting earlier in the day with the minister.

Marion wondered how he would feel when he found out that Walker had escaped. Once the alarm was raised, it would definitely make the newspapers, as Walker would be the first boy to escape under her father's captainship of the Nautical School Ship *Sobraon*. Many years ago, boys had often gone over the side at night, but back then the ship was moored within swimming distance of dry land.

The party began to break up and guests were escorted up on deck. Marion hung back, fretting about how to tell her father what she had seen and the code she had cracked.

Under the fairy lights the guests, including Mrs Crosscapel, were handed down the gangway to meet the cutters manned by the boys. They would be rowed to Cockatoo Island and from there catch the ferries waiting to take them back to the Circular Quay.

Mr Tart was the last to leave. He shook Marion's hand before getting into the boat. Marion stood with her father and Mr Mason, watching as the rowboats raced each other to Cockatoo Island. The trip was a short one, and soon the guests had disembarked at the wharf and the boys were rowing back to the ship.

The boys hauled the cutters up for the night at the *Sobraon*'s sides, saluted the captain and the lieutenant, wished them good night, and then headed off to their hammocks. Marion watched as they strode past. There was Salt and Bell. There was Williams and Sumner. And there was—Alexander Walker!

Marion started. It was definitely him. His shoulders were slumped and he looked exhausted. His damp uniform clung to him and his hair was slick and dark with water. He felt her gaze and looked slightly worried, but then triumph shone in his eyes and he straightened up and hurried past her.

CHAPTER 10

# MRS CROSSCAPEL RUNS RIOT

Three weeks passed, and January turned into February. The time before Marion would begin lessons again was fast dwindling. She dreaded starting at a new school, but she was looking forward to making new friends.

Agnes was probably only days away from arriving in Southampton in England before going on to Paris, and Marion hoped she'd soon receive a letter from her, posted at one of the ports along the way. She was frustrated that Agnes hadn't written yet, but now that disappointment was turning into excited anticipation. *A letter must come soon!* she thought.

Over the last three weeks, more and more boys had returned to the ship, their apprenticeships cut short by bad behaviour.

Through the closed door to her father's office, Marion had heard reports of stolen livestock, thefts from stores in small country towns, and burglaries at local residences.

Every day brought a returned pupil on board, and each time Marion felt the captain's sense of shame as the boy grinned and waved to his friends. It was a mystery why they were coming back in such numbers and why the lessons the staff were teaching on board no longer had any effect.

What Marion knew for sure was that it was linked to Alexander Walker. She was a little wary of him, especially as the boys on the ship were under his spell. They scuttled out of Walker's way when he came on deck. They deferred to him in class, and they offered to carry his books. During cricket matches on Cockatoo Island he was always the bowler, and when he tired of the game it quickly broke up. Some of the younger boys asked the ship's barber to cut their hair just like Walker's, but the man refused. And even Norman Roth, who was still in class seven, didn't shoulder Walker or roll his eyes at him like he did the others.

Marion's desire to stay away from the boys only increased. Apart from Henry Edwards, the boys were still unkind to her, so she kept to her room.

Marion was now sure Walker had left the ship on the night of the Lantern Talk, so she was on the lookout in case it happened again. She still didn't know why he'd left the ship, where he had been, who he had met, or why he had come back. But three weeks had passed and Walker had not gone missing again.

During that time, her father had become more and more anxious. His eyes no longer twinkled, the buttons on his coat were unpolished, and he'd taken his anger out on Marion more than once. He'd even grounded her when she refused to go to Cockatoo Island to play. 'All you do is sit in your room and fret—you must come out!' he'd said.

As punishment, she had been barred from reading in her room and forced to dust her mother's ornaments in the sitting room. She had dusted dozens of gaudy ladies in frilly dresses. It was boring, but it hadn't inspired her to go outside.

Then one day, at her father's behest, Mr Mason sought her out and encouraged her to come up on deck to help him with a visitor. She resented it for a moment, then he showed her a bright purple visitor's ticket for a tour of the floating school. She recognised the name on it—*Mrs Crosscapel.* It was enough to finally lure her out into the sunshine.

And there was Mrs Crosscapel, standing on deck in the same clothes as last time, an urgent look in her eyes. 'Ah,' she said when she spotted Marion, the corners of her mouth turning down, 'it's the girl who stuck to me like glue last time!'

Marion found the comment suspicious, but Mr Mason seemed more interested in admiring how pretty Mrs Crosscapel was.

'Now, Lieutenant Mason,' Mrs Crosscapel said, holding her hair down as a breeze whipped up, 'I should like a tour of this ship from top to bottom. I am interested in *every* aspect of the place.'

Marion frowned. Normally only journalists asked for such a tour. 'Why are you so intrigued by the ship?' she asked.

For the second time, Mrs Crosscapel looked seriously annoyed. 'I was under the impression that this institution *warmly* accepts visitors,' she said to Mr Mason. 'Perhaps I was wrong?'

'Of course we do, Mrs Crosscapel,' Mr Mason assured her, casting a disapproving glance at Marion. 'Everyone is welcome.

Miss Neitenstein will take you around the deck while I fetch the visitors' book for you to sign. I will be back momentarily.' He lifted his cap and disappeared into the depths of the ship.

'Where are the pupils?' Mrs Crosscapel asked sternly.

'In lessons, madam, or working below decks. It's a school day.'

'I wish to see them. *Now.* Each and every one of them.'

Marion hesitated. 'Maybe we should wait for Mr Mason. Tours are not allowed to interrupt school lessons, you see. Normally, we just take people around—'

Mrs Crosscapel was not listening. She picked up her long skirts and hurried towards the steps leading down into the ship. Marion looked around desperately, then followed her at pace along the corridor.

Captain Neitenstein stepped out of his office at the precise moment Marion passed his quarters and she hurtled headlong into him.

'Marion!' he cried. 'Where are you hurrying to?'

'It's Mrs Crosscapel—I've lost her!'

'The visitor? Where did she go?

Marion pointed down the hallway. The captain strode off after Mrs Crosscapel, with Marion bringing up the rear.

'Where might she have headed?' the captain asked over his shoulder.

Marion shrugged and followed her father as he moved methodically through the rooms. It soon became obvious where Mrs Crosscapel was, as raucous sounds from the schoolroom echoed through the vessel. Father and daughter hurried towards it.

'Madam!' Mr Leer called out over the boys' shouts and catcalls, '*Madam*! I really must insist that you—'

'Julian!' came Mrs Crosscapel's desperate voice. 'Julian Crosscapel! You *must* be here.'

The captain threw open the door to the schoolroom and most of the boys fell silent. Only those who had recently been returned from their apprenticeships kept talking. There were sniggers as a boy at the back of the room cruelly mimicked Mrs Crosscapel's call.

The room was in chaos. The blackboard had been overturned and Mr Leer was covered in chalk. The boys' books were strewn across the floor, and several inkwells had been upset in the commotion. Mrs Crosscapel was moving across the front of the room, swallowing back tears as she peered into each boy's face.

'My boy!' she cried. 'He must be here. You must have seen him. He's clever—' she tapped her head.

'Enough!' the captain boomed. 'You have disturbed this lesson long enough!'

But Mrs Crosscapel was not listening. Having searched every boy's face, she turned and fled into the library behind the schoolroom, seeking more boys.

The captain strode swiftly between the desks, and the boys at the back of the room whooped again. Mr Leer finally lost his temper. He sent a boy off to find prefects to escort the misbehaving students to the captain's office for punishment.

Marion followed her father. Mrs Crosscapel, still calling out her son's name, was now wreaking havoc in the mess room. Mr Mason appeared from the other end of the hall and hurried towards her. The boys, who were tying knots for their seamanship classes, looked up in surprise as Mr Mason bundled the lady out of the room.

'Really, Mrs Crosscapel, this is unacceptable behaviour. Your visit was granted under certain restrictions. You were to stay with staff at all times,' Mr Mason said as they escorted her along the corridor.

'Quite inexcusable, Mrs Crosscapel,' Captain Neitenstein added.

'My son, my son,' she sobbed. 'I'm sorry, Captain, but he went missing some time ago and he cannot be found. He must be alive! I would feel it here if he'd died,' she said, clasping a hand to her heart. 'He is alive. I *know* it. He was stolen from me by Joseph Bragg who runs the Forty Thieves push,' she stammered. 'This ship takes boys like mine, so I hoped against hope that he would be here. But he's not.' Her head drooped and she sobbed loudly.

'We have never had a boy here called Crosscapel, or anything like it,' the captain assured her.

The lady described her son to them. 'But that was five years ago,' she said. 'He'd have grown up a lot since then.'

'You have seen all our boys now,' Mr Mason said quietly. 'And none of them was him.'

Two prefects moved past them, frogmarching a class-seven

boy from the schoolroom. The captain nodded to them and excused himself.

'I will take Mrs Crosscapel back on deck,' Mr Mason informed the captain as he left. 'Miss Neitenstein, would you mind going down to the sickbay to help Henry Edwards until I get back?'

Mrs Crosscapel looked hopeful for a second, but Mr Mason quickly explained. 'Edwards and the other boy in the sickbay were both abandoned by their mothers. Hardly a match for you, eh?'

Marion made her way down to the sickbay deep within the ship. It had whitewashed walls for easy cleaning, several berths and a seat in the middle of the room for a nurse. The far end contained lockable cabinets where bandages, medicines and new uniforms were stored. The portholes were open wide to allow fresh air in.

As Marion stepped over the threshold, a soft voice asked from deep within a pile of blankets, 'What's all the noise up there?'

'I don't know, but it sounded like a lady yelling,' Henry Edwards replied.

A head emerged from the hammock, and Marion was surprised to see Alexander Walker. His face was pale and his teeth chattered, even though it was the middle of summer, and he was wrapped in blankets. Beads of sweat had formed on his forehead.

Henry saluted her. Jumbo lay curled up on the floor, panting, his eyes following Henry as he limped across the room. 'Walker has come down with a sudden chill, Miss,' Henry told her. He moved to one of the cabinets and reached up with his good hand. 'I've been reading to him,' he added, pointing to a book under the chair he'd been sitting on.

Walker tried to sit up, but then sank back in the hammock. 'Thank you, Miss, for comin' to see me,' he mumbled.

*Why is he being nice to me? He must be delirious*, Marion thought.

'You're like Mr Bragg, carin' for me,' Walker slurred. 'When I was younger he was teachin' me and—' His voice trailed off and he sighed. 'Julian. That lady was looking for Julian.'

Henry gently tucked the blankets in around Walker, who had started coughing. 'He was disturbed from his sleep by that lady, Miss,' Henry explained. 'Is everything alright up above now?'

'Yes. Mr Mason is seeing her off the ship. Walker's right. She was looking for her son, Julian. But he's not here.'

Footsteps sounded in the hall and two prefects entered the room. They removed their caps as they ducked their heads under the low doorframe and stood quietly, waiting for Walker's coughing to subside.

'Walker any better, Edwards?' the taller of the two asked, ignoring Marion.

'Not much,' Henry replied.

'We came to ask if he had any pocket money to donate to the Famine Relief Fund. One of the boys in the schoolroom said he does.'

They both looked expectantly at the boy in the hammock.

Walker's eyes snapped open. 'No,' he croaked, 'I've not got any grey.'

'You sure?' one of the prefects asked. 'One of the boys said you got a good tip last week when you helped the band boys at the Botanic Gardens.'

'*No*,' Walker insisted.

'Look here, Walker, you might be king among the rough boys here, but fair's fair. You got that coin to share with us all. We don't want it for ourselves—it's for our charity donation.'

'I said *no*, didn't I?' Walker cut in, speaking clearly for the first time. 'And don't have a down—I need it for me self—'

'We're not bearing grudges, Walker. And, anyway, what do you want it for?'

'None of your business!'

And there the matter rested, as Walker vomited spectacularly all over the floor. Henry rushed off to fetch a bucket and mop, Jumbo trotting behind him.

Marion stared at Walker. *The boys always pool their money,* she mused. *That's how they got the Magic Lantern and the band instruments. Now Walker has refused for a second time to share his pocket money. What on earth does he need the money for?*

## CHAPTER 11
# THE STOWAWAY

Two days later, there was a knock at Marion's door. It was evening, and she was reading *Oliver Twist* in bed. Even though he could be terrible, she liked the Artful Dodger best out of all of Fagin's boys.

The knock came again. Her mother entered, holding a thick package. The address on the envelope was neatly penned in perfect copperplate cursive:

*Miss M. Neitenstein*

*Nautical School Ship* 'Sobraon'

*Paramatta River, near Cockatoo Island*

*Sydney, Australia*

Marion's eyes lit up. 'Agnes!' she cried. 'Thank you, Mama.'

Marion looked at the envelope with its blob of red sealing wax and noticed that some of the paper had been torn away. 'It's already been opened,' she said.

'It must have been damaged in the post, which happens sometimes. I wouldn't worry about it,' her mother told her as she left the room.

Marion unfolded the pages and began to read.

*Dear Marion,*

*I am writing to you again, but this time we are in Cape Town rather than Sydney. Did you receive my last letter? I had thought that I might have a letter from you waiting for me in port—but none was there. No matter—ships do complicate letter writing so!*

*Mother has been quite thrilled with the voyage so far, and spends most of her time promenading on deck, wearing her different hats and bonnets in the sun. She would be quite tanned if she were not so particular! As you know, she has sailors' blood in her veins and walks about the deck, even in high seas, as though her feet were firmly on land.*

*Father was seasick before we even set sail, and he continues ill even now that we are in port. He looks rather green and walks about with his handkerchief constantly clutched to his lips. Mother calls him a softie and a noodle, but she tries to soothe him with many, many cups of tea. Soon, though, we will be sailing north again, with South America to the west and the great coast of Africa to the east.*

*There are not many other girls our age on the ship, which means that most of my time is spent either playing with the babies on board or using the ship's library. All of the passengers added a volume or two to the library at the start of the journey, and I am currently reading a Mr Legard's copy of* Vanity Fair. *It is very exciting. Perhaps you have a copy too in your ship's library? If you do, do read it, and let me know what you like of it.*

*I miss you so much that it would be a great comfort to me to hear from you. I think of you often—I see the clock and wonder what is happening on your father's ship or I see my pendant and I wonder what you are up to. Do the boys still look forward to the Lantern Talks? Are you being brave and petting the rabbits in the pet sheds without me? I hope so very much.*

*Your closest friend,*

*Agnes*

As she reread the letter, Marion noticed a greasy line running under some of the writing, as though someone with a dirty finger had traced the words as they read them. Marion shivered and tried to banish the thought from her mind. After all, there was no reason for anyone to read her mail.

Shuffling her shoes back on, she headed for the library to borrow some desk space to write back to Agnes. The boys were just starting dinner in the mess room, so Marion found a compartment in the back of the library, secluded from prying eyes. She took a sheet of letter-writing paper emblazoned with the letterhead 'From the N. S. S. *Sobraon*' from the pile in the middle of the desk, withdrew a small bottle of emerald ink from her pocket, chose a red-barrelled pen with a thin italic nib, and dipped the pen in the ink. As the ship shifted on the water, and the noise from downstairs abated while the boys ate their meals, Marion wrote her letter.

*Dear Agnes,*

*I am so happy to have received your letter. I think your first must have been lost somehow. Perhaps it will turn up one day. At the moment it is a mystery where it has gone. Perhaps it is floating somewhere in a post bag in the harbour!*

*I miss you very much. Soon I am to begin at my new school. There was a delay, you see, as some of the buildings sprung a leak in a storm a month ago (the ship tumbled on the waves that night, I can tell you!). They want the girls to stay at home until classes can begin as normal. It means that I am on the ship most days.*

*Mr Mason has me helping in the sickbay at the moment. One of the boys—Walker is his name—has a terrible fever and needs watching in case he worsens and the doctor needs to be sent for. He is a strange boy indeed. He is rough like so many of them, and I heard one boy call him a king among the worst boys—and he is right.*

*Many boys have been brought back early from their apprenticeships due to misbehaviour. Papa is very sad, and angry, about it. I think it's linked to the Forty Thieves push—and Walker. Some of these boys come to visit him in their breaks, checking if there is anything that can be done for his comfort. They ask me often when he will be well again (it is the only thing they say to me as otherwise they pretend I am not there).*

*Walker was sitting up yesterday with a terrible cough. He has awful scars on him. I think he must have had a very hard life. Though I wonder what he has done to make some of the roughest boys love him so.*

*I try sometimes to go to Cockatoo Island, but the boys are unfriendly.*

*Mr Mason thinks that they are shy of me. Only one, Henry Edwards, is kind to me. He told me yesterday, as we nursed Walker, that his sister and I are similar. He said I have the same kindness about me and that I like stories as she did. She died when she was four, hit by a cart on King Street. It is so very sad.*

*I still read a lot. Currently I am reading* Oliver Twist. *I will try and find your* Vanity Fair.

*Tell me soon how the rest of the voyage goes, and when you are due in Paris. Do you think you might send me a picture of your ship, or of London? As you know, one day I would love to visit Europe.*

*Your true friend,*

*Marion*

As Marion signed her name in a loopy signature, she heard footsteps in the library.

'Miss Neitenstein,' Mr Leer said, putting a bundle of odds and ends on the desk, 'are you writing to your friend?'

'Yes, Agnes' letter finally arrived! Are there any spare envelopes? There are only writing sheets left on the table here.'

Mr Leer hurried off to the classroom, where he had a small stash in his desk.

The ship tilted, and the ropes and rigging strained above her. Suddenly, a gust of wind whipped through an open porthole. Shivering, Marion got up and clamped it shut.

The wind had scattered Mr Leer's belongings across the floor, and Marion bent down to gather them up. A piece of paper was caught on a ball of twine. Untangling it, Marion spotted twelve familiar ink blots. They were identical to those in the message she had deciphered on the night that Walker escaped from the ship and then inexplicably returned.

'Mr Leer!' she called, shoving the note in her pocket and hiding her letter to Agnes in a book on a shelf behind her. 'Sorry, I've got to go. I'll collect an envelope from you later, if I may,' and she ran out of the library.

Heart hammering, Marion skidded down the stairs. At the bottom she steadied herself, then hurried off along the corridor to the sickbay. The door was ajar and she pushed it open. Henry was at the cabinet, cleaning up. Jumbo sat nearby, gazing fondly at him. But the hammock where Alexander Walker had been for several days was empty.

'Where's Walker?' Marion asked, panicking.

Henry shrugged. 'He said he was feeling better and wanted to go up to dinner. I tried to stop him, but he was steady enough on his feet, so I let him go. I didn't want a row about it. And Mr Mason is up there, so he'll send him back down if he needs to.'

Marion was already in the corridor. She heard Henry calling her name as she climbed the stairs, but she kept going. She rushed to her room, pulled a thick jumper over her head, retied her boots with double knots and dashed out. Reaching the deck, she looked around. She couldn't see or hear anyone, so she tiptoed into the shadow of the quarterdeck. Nearby she heard the slither of a rope unfurling, followed by the sound of a rowboat being carefully lowered into the water. Whoever it was, they were unsteady on their feet and breathing hard.

Slipping into the shadows around the ship's mainmast, Marion looked over the rail. A jolly boat floated beside the gangway. Someone in a sailor suit was busy recoiling a rope. While he was distracted, Marion tiptoed down the gangway. She slid into the jolly boat and hid under the tarpaulin at its bow.

She lay there, hardly daring to breathe. The boat lurched as Alexander Walker climbed in. She knew it was him. His teeth were chattering, and he stifled a cough as he pushed the boat away from the ship and began rowing east.

# CHAPTER 12
# SEWERS CANAL

Sydney Harbour was a busy place in the evening, and no one gave a second glance at a boy in a rowboat all by himself. Under the musty tarpaulin, Marion listened to the putt-putt of other watercraft and the oars slicing through the water. Walker's bouts of rowing were powerful but not long lasting. Every few minutes he stopped to rest and let the boat drift closer to its destination. Then he'd cough and begin rowing again with vigour.

Marion's mind was buzzing with questions. *What was driving Walker to keep going? Surely he could put things off until he was better. And who was sending the ink blur messages? Why did they have no sympathy for Walker when he was so very ill? Can I prevent*

*Walker's escapes and put a stop to the growing feeling of unease on the ship? Does all this strange activity have anything to do with the boys returning to the ship from the countryside?*

After almost an hour of rowing, Walker found a jetty. The noises of the city were louder now. From her hiding place, Marion heard the calls of drunken men on the wharf, the rattle of cartwheels on cobblestones, children cackling and adults quarrelling. As Walker clambered out of the boat and secured it to the wharf, Marion kept very still.

Marion peeped out from under the covering. Walker paused, and then moved off quickly across the wooden slats of the jetty. He looked uncertainly around, his hands thrust in his pockets. Spying a familiar landmark, he straightened up and set off more confidently than before.

Marion was out of the boat in a flash, following close behind him. The sun was starting to set, and she felt vulnerable as she moved out of the port and into what she realised was The Rocks. Marion shivered. She had never been here before, but she knew it was a famous slum where many criminals lived.

A hand suddenly reached out and stroked her jumper. Marion flinched as a skinny waif of a girl with bulging eyes and lank, knotted hair grabbed onto her sleeve. Marion tried to push her away while still keeping sight of Walker.

'Maud!' a woman shouted. The girl stopped dead. The woman was swinging a half-empty bottle in her hand, and she took a swig before speaking again. 'Leave the maid alone. We've gotta find somewhere to put our heads down or I'm like to fall down.' Then, after a moment, the woman added, 'Hah!'

A man stumbled out of a nearby doorway and called out to the woman, 'Ya' don't have a down on me—'

'Ugh, Ned, you don't know who's which from when's what. Get away from me!' She lashed out at the man. He tried to duck, but the bottle hit him on the head. He grunted, stumbled and grasped his temple. The woman inspected the unbroken bottle, cackled and drank deeply from it. She beckoned to Maud. The girl took one last hungry look at Marion, then skipped off on her bare feet down a nearby alley. The man slumped down in the gutter.

Marion hesitated. She yearned for her cosy room with its handmade quilt and the mug of warm cocoa beside her bed. She was tempted to hide in the boat and wait for Walker to return, but that wouldn't help her father. She needed to uncover Walker's secret. So she jogged along, following Walker, who was now far ahead of her.

Around her, gangs of children roamed free, shoeless and in rags. Men and women coughed and slurred and spluttered as they were thrown out of pubs, reeking of drink and sweat. An open door on Argyle Street revealed a haze of strange-smelling smoke.

*Is that one of the opium dens Mr Tart is trying to shut down?* Marion wondered. It was another world.

Walker turned right at the end of Argyle Street, and as Marion turned the corner she could see the masts of ships and ferries in the harbour. He turned onto George Street, looking around to check he wasn't being followed. Marion hid in the shadows of a building.

She'd often walked along George Street, but always at the other end where the respectable shops were located, like Mr Tart's tearooms. *This* end of George Street was full of derelict buildings. Here families lived in houses with collapsed roofs and rotting floors. The stench outside one house made Marion retch. It was a horrible mixture of rotting food and sewage. She pressed her handkerchief to her nose and hurried on.

Marion followed Walker down George Street, and then he suddenly disappeared. She blinked and hurried forward. This part of the street was fronted by pubs and boarding houses, their lights glowing behind frosted doors. A man on the opposite side of the street watched her closely as he smoked in the doorway of a house. She dared not ask him if he'd seen Walker.

A gang of noisy boys was heading in her direction. Following them was a group of chattering girls. They tried to drape their arms around the boys at the back of the group but were brushed off. Marion stepped aside to avoid them.

'This one's a big one. Bragg wants us all there,' she heard one of the boys say.

'Sewers Canal ain't Forty Thieves territory,' another boy told him.

'Yeah, but the Argyle Cut push is lettin' Bragg use it.'

'In their interest,' responded another, tapping the side of his nose and winking.

Marion flattened herself against the wall as they pushed past her. The boys didn't look twice at her, but the girls did, screwing up their faces and looking her up and down.

'Drab,' one laughed, and another agreed, adding, 'Not quite a pennorth of treacle, eh?'

Marion ignored the comments and followed them as they entered Sewers Canal. The alleyway was about a yard wide, a narrow space thieved from between two large buildings. It was claustrophobic and smelt awful. Marion followed the group along the alleyway, trying to breathe through her mouth.

The others were carousing now, the girls singing a song and trying to goad the boys into joining in.

One of the boys slapped the girl nearest him. 'Mary,' he said, 'you know how many to a dozen, so be sharp and shut it. Bragg'll want quiet so he can think.'

Mary was stunned into silence. The other girls learned the lesson too and proceeded without talking.

Tagging along behind them with her head down, Marion found herself in a large warehouse. The cavernous space was filled with toppling boxes and crates. Lamps were strung along the walls, but they did little to illuminate the space.

Dozens of boys and girls had crowded into the building. Some were very young indeed, while others were almost adults. They lazed about, draping themselves over the boxes, laughing and swearing. Those who did move around the room shuffled and sloped, dragging their feet. Very few of them had shoes. Marion, in her jumper and boots, felt conspicuous, so she stationed herself near the open door.

Every now and then a boy whistled and someone on the other side of the room gestured back, in what Marion assumed to be some kind of code. A girl near her spat on the ground and tried to rearrange her greasy locks with her fingers. Everyone was filthy, and their clothes didn't fit. They were either too short, with trousers flapping around ankles and vests exposing thin bellies, or too long, with sleeves covering hands and feet tripping on coat-tails. Marion thought of the difference between them and the well-fed boys on the *Sobraon* in their neat sailor suits.

She scanned the room. A throne-like chair had been placed at the far end, in a raised area like a stage. The wing-chair's cushions sagged a little and it had been mended none too carefully, but it was clearly intended to look majestic.

A boy rushed into the hall through the backdoor. 'No coppers,' he announced.

A hush fell over the hall, and Marion waited nervously for something to happen. A thin curtain twitched near the throne and a figure emerged. He wore a gentleman's frockcoat with a dark brown, ominous stain down one side. His boots were fashionable but unpolished, and a grubby neckerchief was tied around his neck like a noose. But it was his eyes that frightened Marion. No wonder a dog, tethered by a rope to the wrist of a boy near her, began whining.

Joseph Bragg's dark, hooded eyes narrowed as he took his place on the throne. He was eating an apple and the audience waited, hardly breathing, as he chewed. He took a final bite, tossed away the core, then spat the final mouthful onto the ground, wiping his lips with his sleeve and grimacing.

'Nugget!' he called. A small boy stepped forward. 'You light-fingered boy, you're quite excellent at lifting *fruit*.' He paused and stroked the boy's face almost affectionately. 'But when you steal, make sure it's quality, not the *tripe* I have here tasted. Here, try for yourself.' Bragg indicated the mushed apple on the floor with salvia bubbling around it. 'Please, taste a little.

Allow yourself to be tempted.'

There was silence as the whole company watched Nugget squat, scoop up the mush and reluctantly put it in his mouth.

'Not nice, is it, my child?'

'Naw,' Nugget responded, forcing himself to swallow. He winced.

'And you'll do better next time, God willing—or you'll end up like Hankley.' Bragg pointed to the bloodstain on his coat. Nugget swallowed hard and scrambled to sit back down in the safety of friends.

It struck Marion that, though Joseph Bragg was dressed like a gentleman, it was just a disguise. His manners were gross. He sniffed and sneezed and spat as he prowled around, looking for someone else to devour. Marion looked closer. Besides Bragg's neckerchief, he had a piece of rope around his neck, which looked like a noose. She shivered, thinking of the men who were hanged by the neck until they were dead at Darlinghurst Gaol for crimes like murder.

She peered around her. There was an atmosphere of keen excitement as the children gazed at Bragg with admiration on their faces. Marion couldn't understand it. She stepped back so the wall was directly behind her and she felt safer. No matter how hard she looked, she couldn't find Alexander Walker. She feared she'd come to the wrong place and would be left stranded in The Rocks. But she knew that if she tried to leave now she'd draw attention to herself.

'What have I been doing recently, my children?' Bragg asked, pacing before them with his hands behind his back, like a teacher explaining a lesson. 'Why, going to and fro on the earth and walking up and down upon it.' He laughed—a bark-like sound that exposed his yellow teeth. The mirthful expression did not reach his eyes.

'Many of my *favourites* are here tonight,' he went on in a harsh whisper, 'at great personal cost.' He nodded to a group of sneering boys in the crowd. 'But, of course, so many of my thieves languish on that *ship*.' Bragg spat out the word. 'They're imprisoned by Dutchy who would take them from *me*—their very *father*!' Bragg slapped his chest twice.

To Marion, Bragg seemed as far away from being fatherly

as it was possible to be. His so-called children were hungry, wild, neglected and poor.

'Those boys cannot be here with us tonight. But I will see them soon. Shortly, shortly.'

'Burn the ship!' a small boy with a vicious expression screamed, jumping up and down on the crate he was standing on. Others echoed his call. All around the room, children clapped and stomped their feet. Those nearest to Marion noticed that she wasn't joining in. They moved away from her, suspicious looks on their faces. Marion started clapping.

Bragg raised his hands above his head and the crowd immediately went quiet. He smirked as he saw that their hearts were filled to the brim with his lies. 'My sons and daughters, you warm my heart. Such crooked minds. I have moulded you in my own image!' He clapped his hands together, delighted. 'Yes, Cotterson, we will surely liberate our friends and burn that ship.'

The children screeched and cheered.

Bragg grinned demonically. 'Perhaps I should introduce our guest of honour now. Alexander Walker is here tonight!'

All eyes turned in the direction of the boy who was being

helped to his feet by Bragg. Tall, blonde, in his *Sobraon* uniform, it was indeed Alexander Walker. Marion shrank as close as possible to the wall.

'You've come in costume, Walker,' Bragg said, grinning. 'A little joke, a jest, my dear.' He turned to the crowd. 'How weak he is. The contaminating influence of Dutchy and his men can suck the life out of even one as great as Alexander Walker.'

Bragg allowed Walker to sit on the edge of his throne for a moment. He laid his hand on the boy's shoulder in the way a proud parent might. 'What goes on in that foul school?' Bragg asked, his face close to Walker's.

Walker coughed several times.

'That's the ticket, the very ticket,' encouraged Bragg. 'Cough up all that rot, my child.'

'It's all school lessons with the masters and chores,' Walker began weakly, his eyelids heavy. 'They keep fast to the timetable. But it's not so hard to slip away and pull the string proper. How else would I have got here tonight?'

There were a few titters in the audience.

'Is Dutchy feeling the heat over our friends returning to the ship?' Bragg asked.

'Yes. The Education Minister, Mr Inglis, comes often to threaten him. He's on the square, sure. Sometimes Dutchy looks like he might scalp him.'

Bragg bared his teeth in delight.

'No one has really twigged that they're all our boys.' Walker paused to catch his breath. 'What are you planning, Mr Bragg? I wish you'd tell us. We want to help.'

Bragg paced away from him, throwing his arms up in irritation. 'In time,' was his only reply.

Marion's eyes burned. *'We want to help.' How could Walker say such a thing?* She felt fiercely protective of her father and the *Sobraon*, and a hatred of Walker bubbled inside her.

Bragg paced around the stage. All eyes were on him as dozens of children hung on his every word. He gestured at Walker. 'What have you brought for me?' he asked, without looking at him.

*He sounds like a spoilt child*, Marion thought.

Walker stood and rummaged in his pockets. With difficulty, he withdrew his hands. Cupped in them were various treasures. He offered them to Bragg, who fished through them greedily.

Marion watched closely. There were the silver coins Walker

had refused to share with the *Sobraon* boys, along with several brass buttons, her mother's white lace handkerchief and Mr Mason's pipe.

Bragg grinned. 'That all?' he asked, his bloodshot eyes fixed on the boy.

Walker nodded. Bragg said nothing. He turned on his heels and made his way to the opposite side of the stage, where he extracted something heavy from a box. It was a loosely rolled carpet. He cradled it in his arms, shook it out flat and then positioned it well away from his throne, making dramatic flourishes with his hands as he did so.

Many of the children began to squirm, glancing sideways at their friends. Near Marion, a boy hissed, 'Aww gawd, it's the Killing Carpet!'

Walker, however, seemed unconcerned.

Bragg surveyed the crowd. 'Master Walker, you are the acknowledged prince of my little kingdom. Look how they love you!'

The thief master moved behind Walker, placed his hands on the boy's shoulders and squeezed tight. A few children chanted Walker's name. Others looked worried. Marion wasn't sure what was going on.

Walker looked exhausted. He perched on the edge of the throne as Bragg's hands ran down his arms. The chanting continued, with more children ignoring the carpet and joining in. And then Bragg plunged a hand into one of Walker's pockets. There was a small struggle and Bragg whipped his hand up high.

Marion gasped. There it was—held tight in Bragg's hand—her missing gold pendant. It had been in Walker's pocket all along. Bragg held it up, swinging it to and fro before Walker's face, as though he was trying to hypnotise him. Walker turned pale and coughed weakly.

'What's this that you keep back, Walker?' The warehouse was completely silent now. 'Is it not the rule of my house that *everything* gained is delivered to me? Hmm? Not a difficult instruction to follow. Especially for my *prince*.'

The gold pendant continued to swing in front of Walker's eyes. He looked sick.

'Not many girls with necklaces on the *Sobraon*, eh?' Still no one moved. 'But there is something more interesting by a *long* way, Walker. And that's not why you stole it but then decided to keep it from me. That's easy—guilt for stealing a pretty girl's best trinket. No, far more intriguing is why the owner of that necklace has decided to attend our little gathering tonight.'

## CHAPTER 13

# THE KILLING CARPET

The colour drained from Walker's face as his eyes darted around the crowd, looking for her.

'Miss Neitenstein!' Bragg called out. 'Would you mind joining us at the front of the room?'

The boys and girls nearest Marion parted to let her through. But Marion hesitated, as dozens of faces turned towards her. She could hear them hissing, 'Dutchy's kid!'

'Hurry, now, child. Don't make me ask again,' Bragg said in a menacing voice.

The door behind her was blocked by angry boys and girls. There was no choice. Marion moved slowly through the crowd as though a magnet were drawing her forward. Her heart thrashed around in her chest.

'Does your father approve of your tardiness?' Bragg joked, showing off his uneven teeth as she reached the stage. Once Marion was near enough, he seized her roughly by the shoulders. She could feel Walker's eyes on her as Bragg steered her backwards onto the Killing Carpet, next to him.

'Mr Bragg,' Walker pleaded, 'honest, I didn't hold back the necklace. It was stuck in my pocket. I wanted to give it to you and I forgot about it. I've not gone soft on the ship. Otherwise, why would I have come here tonight?' He swallowed loudly. 'I'm loyal. I've suffered to serve you on that ship.' A coughing fit stopped his pleading.

'Stop talking, Walker!' yelled Cotterson, the boy who wanted to burn the ship.

'Yeah!' called another, spitting nosily on the ground.

'You're a traitor!' shouted another.

Several children nodded in agreement.

Walker's face was pale, his mouth opened in shock. Boys who had been chanting out his name a moment ago were now turning on him.

Bragg grinned. 'How the tide turns,' he gloated, eyeing

Walker closely under a heavy brow.

'Why'd you bring *her* here?' yelled a girl in the crowd.

'I didn't!' Walker retorted to the mass of outraged children. 'She must've followed me. She watches me all the time, and she must've worked it out. She's clever.' Walker glanced at Marion. 'But she won't say nothin'. Just let her go. She'll keep her trap shut.' Walker looked meaningfully at her. 'Won't you, Miss?'

Marion nodded vigorously.

But Bragg was shaking his head too. 'She's seen too much.' He shook a finger at Marion. 'You're from a world of books and scones and tea, my dear, and you should *not* have come here tonight.'

Marion could not take her eyes off the bloodstains on Bragg's coat. There were other marks on it too, and she wondered how many people's final moments were represented there. Beside her, she felt Walker shaking. He'd turned a shade of green, as though he might vomit again. Marion felt the same, but not because she was ill.

'My father knows I'm here,' she said in as brave a voice as she could muster.

Bragg laughed. 'You're a liar, Miss Dutchy.' His pitiless eyes bored into hers. 'You're a stowaway, and now you're up to your neck in it.'

He suddenly stopped talking and waved his hands for silence. Far away beyond the warehouse came the faintest sound of a whistle. Bragg flicked his head, and two boys at the back of the room headed off to check it out.

The noise was becoming louder and getting closer. Quick footsteps sounded beyond the walls. Marion's heart was fit to burst. The children were shushing each other as they strained to hear.

'Bleedin' coppers!' came the shout from one of the boys who had headed outside. 'RUN!'

There was a stampede for the doors, with children climbing over each other to get out.

Bragg was not ready to leave. From his sleeve, he produced a long knife. He clicked his fingers, and two large boys grabbed Marion and Walker from behind, binding their arms. Bragg advanced on them, and Marion began screaming and kicking.

And then Walker shuddered and projectile vomited. The boy holding him sprang back to avoid the spray, and Walker collapsed on his knees. In the confusion, Marion's foot connected with

Bragg's wrist and the knife fell to the floor. Bragg cursed and clutched his arm.

Marion seized Walker's hand, pulled him up and dragged him towards the door. Bellowing for them to stop, Bragg made to follow. But then he thought better of it and vanished behind the curtain with his two helpers, keen to evade the police.

The scene out on the street was chaotic. The police were rounding up the children who'd escaped from the warehouse and bundling them into vans. They didn't notice two small figures slink along Harrington Street and disappear up Argyle Street.

Walker breathed unevenly as Marion led him back to the wharf, dodging past drunken sailors and catcalling women. He could barely stand, and she had to half carry him, his arm around her shoulders and her arm around his waist. She helped him down into the jolly boat and wrapped the tarp around his shoulders to keep him warm. A clock nearby struck seven as Marion uncoiled the rope, tossed it into the jolly boat and pushed off from the wharf.

Her knees were shaking and her stomach felt like it was home to several dozen butterflies, but Marion took the oars and began rowing back to the ship. It was tough work, and she had to stop every now and then to catch her breath. Sometimes the oars just splashed on the surface of the water and she made no ground at all. It was frustrating. Rowing looked so easy when she watched the boys do it. But after a while she found her rhythm.

The sun had disappeared by the time Walker awoke. 'Where are we?' he croaked, peering around blearily.

'Almost at the *Sobraon*,' she said, pointing into the darkness, where the hull loomed up before them.

Marion wondered how they could get back onboard the ship without being seen. She knew she'd be in a lot of trouble if her father discovered what she'd done.

Walker appeared to be thinking along the same lines. 'Can you swim?' he asked. Marion nodded. 'Then brace yourself!' Walker took a hammer out of a box under the bench and began to hack holes in the bottom of the wooden boat.

'What are you doing?' squealed Marion, as water rushed

through the holes. She scrambled away from it, knocking an oar overboard.

Walker ignored her. He stood up. 'Come on,' he said, and plunged into the water.

Marion had no choice but to follow him as the boat was already sinking. She gasped as the cold water enveloped her.

Walker trod water beside her, trying to keep his eyes open. 'You alright?' he asked.

'Are you?'

He nodded, reached out and grasped the neck of her jumper, intending to pull her along. She wriggled free. 'I can swim just fine on my own,' she told him as the jolly boat disappeared under the water.

'Hey!' Walker called, looking up at the deck far above them and waving his arms. 'Help!'

Marion joined in. At first there was no reply, and then the worried face of Mr Mason appeared over the edge of the railing. It took a moment for him to understand what he was seeing.

'Blimey,' he said, snatching the cap off his head. 'Man overboard!' he called urgently to someone on the deck. 'And *girl* overboard too!'

Two life buoys were thrown over the side, and Marion and Walker paddled over to them. Mr Mason and one of the prefects stood on the gangway, reeling them in.

Marion was hauled up first. Another prefect appeared with blankets for them both. There were shouts, and lights suddenly blazed in several portholes.

'Find the captain and his wife. Tell them their daughter's been located,' Mr Mason ordered. 'Miss Neitenstein, did you fall in? Walker, did you see her go over and dive in after her?'

Walker blinked slowly as he sat there, dripping onto the platform. He cradled his face in his hands for a moment and then looked up at Mr Mason.

'Other way around, sir—Miss saved *me* tonight.' And with that, he fainted.

## CHAPTER 14

# THE LOST PENDANT

Marion's mother, a look of terror on her face, appeared at the railing. A shawl covered her nightdress and her hair fell in dark tendrils down her back. She hurried down the sloping gangway, grabbed Marion and hugged her close.

'Your daughter deserves a medal, madam,' Mr Mason told her, as he scooped Walker up in his arms. 'Walker here was delirious and he fell over the rails into the water. Miss Neitenstein heard the splash and dived in to rescue him. She saved his life.'

Marion pushed her wet hair out of her eyes and stole a glance at Walker. One of his arms dangled limply and his head lolled to the side. She wanted to go with him to the sickbay and find out what was going on, but her mother put an arm around her shoulder and guided her up the gangway.

'Come, my dear girl,' she said. 'We must get you out of those wet things.'

In Marion's room, her mother helped her struggle out of her wet clothes. She handed her a towel and a clean nightdress then bustled out of the room. When she returned with a steaming cup of tea and a plate of biscuits, Marion was already in bed, snuggled under the covers.

'Are you sure you're not hurt?' her mother asked. Marion shook her head. 'Then drink your tea and get some sleep, my dear.' Her mother kissed her goodnight, tiptoed out and closed the door.

Marion stared at the hook on the back of the door. The events of the night flashed before her. The letter to Agnes, secreted in one of the books in the library. The ink blurs on the note. The horrible children in Sewers Canal. The murderous look in Bragg's eyes. The pendant that Walker had stolen, gone now forever. The bloodstains on Bragg's coat. The vicious faces of the children when they turned on Walker. The Killing Carpet she'd been forced to stand on.

*Walker is no longer Joseph Bragg's favourite. Is he in danger? Am I?* Marion wondered as she shivered under the bedclothes. She tried to settle herself by listening to the familiar, comforting sounds of the ship around her. Soon all would be quiet. *But is that what I want?* she asked herself. *And do I really want to be alone?*

She vaulted out of bed and placed a chair under the door handle. If someone tried to get into her room, at least the scrapping noise would give her some warning. She checked that her porthole was locked, and then, feeling rather childish, looked under her bed.

Satisfied that all was well, Marion slipped between the covers again. She knew that officers patrolled the deck at night. *Surely they'll raise the alarm if anyone tries to board the ship*, she thought. To calm herself, she sipped the lukewarm tea and ate the biscuits. But she was still too scared to turn down the lights and sleep.

Her brain was busy processing what had happened. *Mr Mason thinks I dived in when Walker fell overboard. He said I deserve a medal. Papa will be proud of me, but it's not the truth. I ran away and put myself in danger. I might never have got back home! And those terrible boys suggested to Bragg that they should burn the ship. Is that really the plan?*

Marion cast about for something to help stop the thoughts swirling around in her head. She picked up the morning's newspaper and read about the troubles in parliament. Then she scanned the advertisements and the classifieds. The headline 'Missing Friends' caught her eye, and she read on.

**Frederick Anlaby Legard, left Ganton, Yorks., about 1852, and came to Victoria as a teacher. It is said that he came to Sydney, New South Wales, after living in Melbourne some years, but inquiries have failed to trace him. Information to Col. James Legard, Kirby Misperton, Yorks.**

But it was the next one that really got her attention.

**A boy, Julian Crosscapel, thirteen years old, was taken from the home of his mother in Balmain five years ago.**

**He has fair hair and brown eyes, and a curious pattern of freckles on his right shoulder. Reason to suspect that the boy is unaware his mother is searching for him. Handsome reward for information as to his whereabouts. Information gladly received by Mrs Crosscapel, c/o the Sydney PO.**

*Poor Mrs Crosscapel*, Marion thought. And with that, she finally fell asleep.

The next morning Marion awoke with a start. The lamps were still burning brightly in her room, and sheets of newspaper were caught up in her bedcovers. She neatly folded the paper and placed it on the table beside her bed.

Once she was dressed, Marion went straight to the library to retrieve her letter to Agnes. She selected an envelope—Mr Leer had restocked the pile in the centre of the table—

and addressed it. She was about to go to the mail bag when she ran into her father and a man she had not met before.

'Here she is!' the man cried. He wore a long cloak and a kind expression. 'It's the heroine of the hour, I believe.'

Her father beamed at her from under his bushy eyebrows. 'Marion, this is Mr Fosbery, the Inspector-General of Police,' he told her. 'He's investigating the theft of our jolly boat last night.'

Marion's blood ran cold. She'd forgotten about that. It was now at the bottom of the harbour, holes in its planks.

'The tale of your daring rescue certainly caught my attention,' Mr Fosbery said. 'It's a far more interesting topic than a little boat going missing,' Mr Fosbery's eyes twinkled but her father looked displeased. 'But don't let on to your father,' the inspector-general added in a loud whisper.

Fosbery delved into one of his pockets, a thoughtful look on his face, and withdrew a small package wrapped in waxed paper. 'Fudge,' he said to Marion. 'From the Loong Shan Tea House. I'm a regular there and Mr Tart gave me this to try. I think it's rather good. Do take the rest and let him know if he should make it a special.' Fosbery winked at Marion and then gestured to her father. 'Now, Captain, take me to where this boat was last seen. We'll see if we can't get to the bottom of it.'

But Fosbery's eyes remained on Marion for a moment, and she had the distinct impression that he was trying to read her mind. Then he strolled off after the captain to investigate the theft.

Marion posted her letter and then ran after them.

'Many boys have returned lately from their apprenticeships,' Fosbery was saying to her father when Marion arrived on deck. 'That is quite unusual, is it not?'

Her father agreed. Fosbery asked the boys' names and the captain reeled them off.

'Why,' the policeman exclaimed, eyes wide, 'they're Joseph Bragg's boys!' Fosbery frowned. He looked at Marion, who was holding a piece of half-eaten fudge. 'Any good?' he asked.

She nodded.

Fosbery winked and looked back at the captain. 'A rough bunch, those thieves. And Bragg's been very active of late. We arrested several of his boys and girls last night.'

Marion gulped, choking on the fudge. Fosbery watched her out of the corner of his eye.

'They were having a rally of some kind. My men broke it up, of course. He was quite far away from his own territory. Surry Hills is the Forty Thieves' patch, not The Rocks. Odd, very *odd.*'

'Who is Joseph Bragg?' the captain asked.

'Thief master of the Forty Thieves,' replied Fosbery. 'Slippery fellow. Never met him myself, actually.'

'Has this anything to do with the theft of our boat?' asked the captain.

'Quite possibly.'

Mr Mason joined them, saluting both the captain and Fosbery. 'Captain,' he began, 'may I borrow your daughter? Walker is still down in the sickbay and getting worse, and I have a group arriving any moment for a tour. Miss, would you mind?'

'Is that the boy you saved last night?' Fosbery asked Marion.

She nodded.

'Then you must take the chance to nurse him now. You might even get a second chance to save his life.' Fosbery chuckled at his own joke. Then he added, his twinkling eyes searching her own, 'Far too much excitement for one day!'

Marion had the distinct impression that Fosbery knew more than he was letting on. *What does he mean by 'too much excitement'?* she wondered. *Does he know I was at The Rocks last night?* She wasn't sure she wanted to leave her father alone with Fosbery. She was worried about what else he might say. But she also wanted to speak to Walker.

Mr Mason headed off to receive the visitors—an old woman accompanied by a stooped old man. The latter had a neckerchief tied jauntily about his throat, and he kept his head bowed and his hands in his pockets.

Marion had no choice but to go below to see Walker. On her way down to the sickbay, she passed several boys. They seemed a little awestruck when they saw her.

'Did she *really* dive in after Walker?' one boy whispered.

'That's what I heard, but what was Walker doing in the water? Apparently he's real sick now, worse than before.'

Marion walked faster.

It was dim in the sickbay. The curtains were pulled across the portholes and there was a stale smell in the air. Marion heard Walker before she saw him. His breath rattled and, even though the room was warm, his teeth were chattering.

She sat down on the stool next to his bed, relieved that he was asleep as she had no idea what to say. This time yesterday he'd been Bragg's thief, a spy sent to her father's ship to report back to the Forty Thieves. He had stolen her most prized possession—her only connection with her friend Agnes who was on the other side of the world. He'd lied, and he'd cheated both her and her father. But he'd also tried to save her life when Bragg made her stand on that terrible carpet. He'd even tried to bargain for her life. And then he'd lied to Mr Mason and made her seem the hero of the hour when they'd been rescued from the water. Marion was not sure what to think of Alexander Walker.

Walker shifted in his sleep, turning onto his side. His whole body convulsed as he coughed. Marion stood up to pull the covers around him. And that's when she saw it—a triangle of freckles on his right shoulder.

Walker stirred. 'Who's there?' he mumbled.

Marion gently pulled the covers up to his throat.

Walker shifted again, turning towards her. His eyes widened when he saw who was standing beside him. 'I'm real sorry for last night, Miss,' he rasped.

Marion said nothing. She didn't know *what* to say.

'I sure wish you hadn't tailed me. It was real stupid to do that. But I'm glad you did,' Walker paused for breath, 'else I wouldn't have gotten back. Bragg would've had me then 'n' there.'

'You're safe on the ship,' Marion replied, although she wasn't entirely sure that was true. Walker swallowed hard and shook his head a little.

'Nah, not safe here. Word will spread sooner than you think. I'm Bragg's enemy now. And so are you. He'll want to find us both as soon as he can.'

Walker began coughing again, his chest rising and falling rapidly as he tried to draw breath. 'Joesph Bragg knows how many to a dozen, Miss. He's sharp and not to be messed with. You saw what he was planning last night.' Walker's eyes rolled. 'I'm too weak, Miss. And this ain't a game.' He swallowed loudly and tried to focus. 'You're a lot braver than I thought you'd be, if I'm honest.'

Walker sighed and his head sank onto his chest, then he rallied again. 'We have to warn the captain about Bragg,' he muttered. 'Danger,' he sighed. 'Look in my pocket. It was on the ground in Sewers Canal.' With that, he fell asleep.

There was a knock at the door. It was Henry and his faithful hound Jumbo. 'Miss, Mr Mason wants you on deck. He asked me to relieve you.'

Marion was relieved Henry didn't ask why she'd rushed out of the sickbay the night before. She picked up Walker's still-damp pants and searched in the pockets.

'Let me take them, Miss, and I'll put them by an open window to dry,' Henry said, holding out his good hand. Marion's fingers folded around something small and cold. She pulled it out and handed the pants to Henry.

'Thank you,' she said, as she hurried out into the corridor.

Once outside the sickbay, she stopped and opened her hand. It was her necklace, of course—the 'trinket' Walker had almost traded for his life.

Marion bit her lip. *Should I tell Papa about The Rocks, Bragg, Sewers Canal and the real reason why we were in the water last night?* she wondered. *If Mr Fosbery is still on board, perhaps I should tell him?* Marion put her head in her hands. *It's all so confusing, and I don't want to get anyone in trouble.*

She hurried up on deck. On the gangway, the captain was farewelling the guests from the ship. Marion watched over the railing as Mr Fosbery assisted the old lady into the rowboat that would convey them to Cockatoo Island.

The humpbacked old man was last to board. He shook her father's hand. 'Thank you for having us, captain,' he said.

Marion peered closer. She knew that voice.

'So lovely to speak with some of your boys,' he continued. 'Such an outstanding job. Just the ticket indeed!'

As the man saluted the captain and stepped onto the jolly boat, his dark, hooded eyes stared up at Marion. It was Joseph Bragg! Marion's guts turned to water.

'Until next time,' he called, smirking.

## CHAPTER 15

# JULIAN CROSSCAPEL

Marion contemplated the words in the classified advertisements—'a curious pattern of freckles on his right shoulder'. She sighed. *There are still so many questions to be answered. Is Alexander Walker actually Julian Crosscapel? Has Bragg told his loyal boys on the* Sobraon *that Walker can't be trusted? Why else would he risk the journey to the ship, right under the noses of Papa and the Inspector-General of Police?*

Marion gripped the railings and watched the boys row Bragg, the old lady and Mr Fosbery away. Though Bragg was off the ship, a sense of menace lingered. She looked around. *Should I come clean and tell Papa everything?* she wondered.

It was the last weekend before her holidays ended. Soon

she would have to deal with a new school, new classrooms, new timetables, new teachers, new lessons and, hopefully, new friends. She was running out of time!

The bugle called and the boys swarmed onto the deck. Usually a muster of the ship's company was quick and efficient, but today it was anything but. Some boys marched in and lined up in the usual organised way, but others meandered slowly to where they were meant to be. Many boys hadn't even bothered to come up on deck yet.

The captain and Mr Mason waited in their usual places on the quarterdeck. Her father pulled his watch from his pocket and checked it.

'Why are the boys so tardy?' he asked. Mr Mason shrugged and shook his head.

The staff down below on the deck were doing their best to get the boys in place, casting worried glances up at the captain. They shouted angrily down the hatches, chiding the other boys for being late. It had little effect.

The large space beside class six was slowly filled by boys in ill-fitting sailor suits. The class-seven boys stood casually, shoulders sagging. Some were messing around with their friends and had to be separated by the prefect Williams. As soon as he turned his back, they began again, mocking him by sticking their noses up in the air and marching on the spot.

Marion stepped forward to get a closer look. Class seven was bigger than ever, its numbers swollen by the badly behaved boys returning in droves from their apprenticeships. These disorderly boys were all members of the Forty Thieves, and it was clear they'd been recalled by Bragg to wreak havoc in the school. Marion wondered what her father would do with them.

The ship's muster was in chaos. Every time her father spoke, the boys in class seven giggled and talked loudly. Even threats from the staff did nothing to stop them. The muster was quickly wrapped up without the usual messages, and the captain dismissed everyone except those in class seven. The staff barred the hatches and ordered the unruly boys to pay attention to the captain.

A hand landed on Marion's shoulder and she jumped. It was Mr Leer. 'Come on, Miss,' he whispered. 'No need to witness this. Your father will deal with those boys. Mr Mason's gone to fetch the cane. Your father doesn't often use violence but, as he said at dinner last night, for some boys brutish behaviour can only be overcome in a brutal way.'

'Would you like to help me with a project?' Mr Leer asked Marion when they reached the library. 'I need to make a Leyden jar, and you are the best person to help, I think. Henry Edwards is also keen.'

Marion followed him into the schoolroom, where Henry was waiting, playing with Jumbo. He waved when Marion arrived.

From the storeroom, Mr Leer collected a crate and placed it carefully on the central teacher's desk. 'A Leyden jar,' he began, pulling a glass jar and some copperleaf sheets from the box, 'collects static electricity. I need to make one now to show some of the boys next week.'

Mr Leer set them each a task. Marion cut up the copperleaf that would line both the inside and outside of the glass bottle. Henry went up on deck to collect seawater in a bucket.

The bottle was lined and covered with copper, then filled with seawater. Mr Leer jammed a cork stopper in the top to seal it and hammered a nail through the cork until it dipped into the fluid.

As Marion watched the copper shine in the light, a group of boys pushed open the schoolroom doors on their way through to the library.

'What's that, sir?' asked one, as his friends wrestled behind him. Marion recognised him as one of Walker's old friends from the Forty Thieves.

'It's a jar that stores static electricity,' Mr Leer replied.

'Are you sure they should be helpin'?' the boy retorted, pointing at Marion and Henry. 'Too dangerous for them to handle, surely?'

But the boy and his friends didn't wait for an answer. They sloped off into the library, making zapping sounds at each other and cackling.

One cried out, 'Imagine if Miss dropped it in the water. She'd electrocute us all!'

Embarrassed, Henry gazed at his feet.

Marion looked from Mr Leer to the contraption and asked, '*Is* it dangerous?'

The teacher laughed. 'Yes and no. If enough static electricity builds up in it, it could give you a nasty shock, but it's not the kind of electricity that would hurt you if you dropped it in the bath with you, for instance. That's *current* electricity, this is *static* electricity. Let me show you.'

From the crate, he pulled out a piece of old woollen blanket and a small glass cup. He rubbed the cloth vigorously against the cup. Marion heard snaps and crackles. Then Mr Leer gently touched the cup to the nail in the Leyden jar.

'Now touch the nail,' he instructed Marion, 'and hold the jar like this.'

Marion followed his instructions, cupping her hand around the wall of the bottle and touching the tip of her index finger to the nail. It sparked and she jumped. She grinned and made way for Henry.

'It zapped me!' Henry cried, jumping up and down.

Mr Leer beamed. 'If I stored too much of the static electricity without touching it and then left it, someone *could* get hurt. So we must be careful.' He gently lifted the Leyden jar back into the crate and put it in the storeroom.

'Will you read to me?' Marion asked Henry.

For a few hours they sat together while Mr Leer marked

exam papers. They broke for lunch, and then returned to reading quietly for the rest of the afternoon.

At about five o'clock, the door to the schoolroom opened.

'Sir, do you know where I might find the captain?' the prefect Salt asked breathlessly. He was holding a blue envelope in his hand. 'This was delivered just now. Urgent, it is.'

Marion stepped forward, offering to take it.

'Thank you, Miss,' the boy replied, and he scurried from the room.

Marion went in search of her father. She found him in his office. He ripped the blue envelope open and quickly skimmed the letter.

'I must go and see the Colonial Secretary immediately,' he told her. 'I'll travel with your mother. The boys are rowing her into town in a few minutes. We won't be back before your bedtime. Let Mr Mason know, will you?' He collected his coat and marched off down the corridor.

Marion found Mr Mason in the sickbay. 'Father's going ashore on urgent business with the Colonial Secretary,' she told him.

'I'll pop back up on deck to see him off and check for orders,

Miss,' he told her. He nodded towards Alexander Walker. 'He's much better now.'

Once Mr Mason had left, Marion moved over to the hammock and looked at Walker. His eyes were closed. She paused, then asked, 'Are you Julian Crosscapel?'

Walker's eyes sprang open. 'What?'

She repeated her question.

'Why are you askin' *me* that?' Walker asked, baffled.

'Because I think you *are* Julian Crosscapel. A lady has been here twice looking for her son. I saw a notice she placed in the newspaper. It said that her son had a curious pattern of freckles on his right shoulder—just like you,' Marion said, blushing. 'She says her son was kidnapped.'

Walker paused a moment to think. He looked very tired. 'Joseph Bragg brought me up,' he said flatly. 'I'm an orphan. My parents died of the fever years ago when I was small. Mr Bragg rescued me from the streets—'

Marion rolled her eyes, and Walker saw red.

'He was the only one to help me, *Miss*. You've lived your whole life with loving parents, a roof over your head and food in your belly. I did too until my parents snuffed it. My father went first. I remember seein' his body. I don't remember my mother's death. I guess they didn't want me to see her corpse.'

Marion stood quietly, her head bowed, her cheeks flushed.

'Mr Bragg scooped me up from the poverty that was about to overtake me, and he fed me and gave me clothes to wear. I had lots of friends there in his little kingdom.'

'But he made you steal,' Marion said.

'Yes,' he said hollowly. 'And much worse besides.'

Marion caught Walker's eye as he spoke, but quickly looked away. *What does 'much worse' mean?* she wondered.

'Okay, you're right,' Walker sighed. 'He *does* use boys and girls as his slaves. When he rolled out the Killing Carpet the other night, I realised how fickle he can be. He doesn't like to be crossed. Gets real angry. But I can't believe he stole me from my ma.'

'I can,' Marion retorted. 'He's a wicked man. Don't you think it's odd that you never saw your mother, that you never went to her funeral? In the notice in the newspaper, Mrs Crosscapel says that her boy might not know who he really is.'

Walker shook his head. 'My ma's dead, Miss.' He was quiet for a moment. 'But thank you for trying to help me.'

Marion thought Walker was about to say something else,

but he didn't. To cover the silence, she thanked him for returning her necklace.

'I shouldn't have filched it in the first place, Miss. I felt bad right away. And then you made me feel even worse when you told me I was selfish not to share Mr Inglis' tip.'

Marion blushed again.

'When I came here, I came as Bragg's spy. He ordered me to get myself arrested, so I put on a bit of a show on King Street and let a man knock me down. But now I want to stay. I like it here. Roth and them others are dim not to see how good we have it.'

'Will you let me write to Mrs Crosscapel? At least you could meet with her.'

'I can't stop you,' Walker said with a shrug.

Marion snatched up a piece of paper. Walker watched as she quickly scribbled a message on it, folded it up and hurried out of the room.

The mail bag was being loaded onto a ferry but Marion caught it in time. The postman promised to rush it to the central post office in Sydney. Relieved, Marion retraced her steps to the sickbay.

As she reached the corridor, she heard an awful ruckus up on deck. There were shouts and loud bangs. It sounded as if something had collided with the *Sobraon*. Marion rushed to a porthole and looked out.

A rotten barge was being tethered to the ship. Its flaking wooden planks grated against the pristine hull of the *Sobraon* as it bobbed about in the swell. Above her, Marion heard the sound of boots on the deck. She frowned. The boys were meant to always be barefooted. Class seven were making trouble again, she was sure.

When she reached the door that led onto the deck, Marion paused and squinted though the frosted glass. She could just make out dozens of boys in ragged clothes rushing about. They were inspecting the rigging, tugging at the ropes, sniffing at the deck, and peering around as though they had never seen such things before.

A smirking boy shuffled past the door, and Marion, hands shaking, quickly turned the key in the lock. It was Cotterson, the boy from Sewers Canal who wanted to burn the *Sobraon*.

Her heart jolted. The barge had delivered the Forty Thieves onto the ship!

As she watched, the mass of children parted and a man made his way along the deck. He stopped right in front of the door. He wore a long frockcoat with a stain down one side, and under his arm was a rolled-up carpet.

Marion didn't dare breathe.

'Tie up the staff!' Joseph Bragg ordered the street urchins around him. 'Liberate my loyal class seven. And then find Alexander Walker and Miss Dutchy, and bring them to me!'

CHAPTER 16

# CHOOSING SIDES

The ship was crawling with children from the Forty Thieves. Marion hunched over so Bragg couldn't see her through the glass and then scuttled down the stairs to the sickbay.

'Bragg is on deck. Get up, quick!' she cried as she burst into the room.

Henry dropped the dish he was holding. 'What did you say, Miss?'

Walker struggled upright and stared at her.

'Joseph Bragg brought his gang with him. They're on deck now. Bragg's looking for us.' Her hand shaking, Marion clicked the lock on the door. 'They'll be here any moment.'

Henry gulped. Walker wrenched himself free of his blankets,

placed his feet unsteadily on the floor and leaned on the table next to him for support.

'You stay in here 'n' hide, Miss,' Henry urged, opening the wardrobe beside him and making room for her among the sailor suits.

Marion took a step forward and then shook her head. 'I've got a better idea. Both of you, turn around,' she said.

The deck was prettily lit, but the illuminated scene was not a happy one. Bragg paced to and fro along the quarterdeck where Captain Neitenstein would normally be during muster. He was wearing the captain's cap and twiddling the captain's cane between his fingers, occasionally thumping it against a canon or a mast as he walked past. Beside him was the unfurled Killing Carpet, silently awaiting its victims. Bragg glanced at it from time to time and smirked.

Nearby, the entire staff of the *Sobraon*, guarded by six of the biggest boys from class seven, were being held, their hands tied behind their backs and ropes lashed around their chests. Mr

Mason had a large bruise on his jaw and his eyes were glazed.

The windows along the deck had been broken and the frosted glass door where Marion had been a few minutes ago had been lifted off its hinges. Mugs and plates were scattered across the deck, and the magic lantern had been smashed, its brass tubes bent and twisted.

Below deck, the fight was just beginning.

In the mess room, the boys from classes one to six were eating their mutton and potatoes, unaware of the events upstairs. The staff had left when they heard a loud bang. As the boys tucked into their meal, they eyed the empty staff table and murmured among themselves.

Finally, two of the prefects rose from their chairs and went to investigate where the staff had got to. As they delivered their dirty plates to the servery on the way out, they were stopped by three boys in sailor suits—Henry Edwards, Alexander Walker and a smaller boy wearing a cap who stared at his feet rather than at those around him.

Before the prefects could say anything, Alexander Walker called out, 'The Forty Thieves are here with Bragg. They've come to destroy the ship! They've got Mason, Leer and the others tied up on deck—'

As he spoke, the doors flew open again and the boys from class seven flooded into the hall. Walker, Edwards and their friend were pushed into the middle of the mess room, swept away from the doors as though a wave had burst into the room.

'Where's the traitor Walker, and Miss?' Norman Roth demanded, as the class-seven boys surged around him.

For a moment, all was quiet. But then a boy stood up and pointed. 'Walker's right there!' he yelled.

There was a scuffle around Walker, as two boys from class seven tried to catch him, while two of the prefects barred their way. Then the boys from the other classes rallied to his side.

'You can't have 'im!' one boy cried. 'Walker's a good lad.'

Another called, 'If he's Bragg's enemy now, then I'm on *his* side!'

Some boys clapped and cheered for the Forty Thieves, while others formed a fence around Walker and his two friends. Some simply backed away.

Roth retreated to the door, murmuring softly to his friends

in class seven as he went. It appeared that they were leaving. Roth even laid his hand on the door handle. But then he spun around and, with the class-seven boys behind him, launched himself at the prefects, Walker and his supporters.

Benches scraped against the floor, plates were used as weapons, and food was thrown around, smattering everyone with peas and gravy.

Marion ducked. Dressed in a sailor suit that was too big for her, and with her hair pinned up under her cap, her disguise had worked so far. But now the boys from class seven were clawing at her, frantic to get hold of her sleeve, her cap, her collar—anything to stop a friend of Walker's leaving the hall. With the help of Walker's fists, Henry's strong right arm, and Marion's kicking feet, she escaped their clutches. Joining hands, Walker, Henry and Marion went ducking and weaving through the crowd in the mess room.

Once they got through the doors, they heard footsteps and catcalls coming along the corridor, so Marion pulled them into the nearby aviary. As she went to shut the door, Jumbo came scurrying down the corridor, searching for Henry.

'Go back, boy,' Henry said, waving at him. 'Don't give

us away!'

Jumbo cocked his head, then sprang away from their hiding place and padded obediently down the corridor.

The three escapees sat hunched over in the closed-in bottom of the birdcage, a finch twittering on its perch above them. Marion had pulled the wooden door shut just as a hoard of Bragg's boys sauntered down the corridor. They heard a strangled bark, a scuffle and the thump of another door closing, then scratching and barking sounds.

Marion turned to Henry, 'It's okay,' she whispered. 'They've just locked him in the storeroom.'

'Girly!' one of the Forty Thieves called out in a sing-song voice alarmingly close to their hideout. 'Where are you, Miss Dutchy?'

The owner of the voice stopped and looked through the netting at the bird above them. 'Aww! Look at the little birdy!' he said. 'Have you seen a girly around here, birdy? My master has a down on that girl after she escaped from Sewers Canal. He wants to put 'er lights out.'

Suddenly, another voice boomed, 'Cotterson, it's on in 'ere. Come on!'

The corridor went quiet, but the din in the mess room got louder.

Marion felt a hand on her shoulder. 'We won't let anyone hurt you, Miss,' Henry whispered.

'I reckon she can look after herself,' Walker responded with a wry grin.

Marion pushed the door open a crack. 'I need to get to my room,' she whispered.

All was clear, so they moved swiftly down the corridor. The sound of the ship's creaking was joined by the ruckus in the mess room and the cries of Bragg's boys. Henry darted off down the hall to the storeroom where Jumbo was clawing at the door.

'The door's locked and we don't have time to get him out,' Walker hissed, waving him back.

Henry shrugged, then disappeared into the schoolroom opposite. He emerged carrying the Leyden jar.

'What the hell do you need that for?' Walker asked.

'It might come in handy,' Henry retorted, hugging it against his chest.

'Come on!' Marion called.

She led them to her father's office. Usually it was neat and tidy, but now there were papers everywhere. The portholes were broken, the leather desktop ripped, the captain's brass navigation equipment broken. Marion noticed her father's cap and stick were missing. He always left them onboard when he disembarked.

With no time to lose, Walker pulled her towards the door behind the chair, which led to her family's private quarters. The Forty Thieves had tried to break through it without success. Luckily, Marion had a key.

Her family's private quarters were untouched by the villains and thieves. The parlour had an oddly serene feel, with its neat chintz armchairs, portraits hanging on the walls and a potted fern next to the piano.

Walker whistled. 'Nice,' he said, gazing around.

Marion's bedroom was next door. She hesitated a moment, wishing she didn't have quite so many dolls on display in their pretty dresses and hats, but there was nothing she could do about it now. She entered the room, pulled down the fishing net, and emptied her dolls onto the bed. Then she threw the net to Walker and they set off for the deck.

Up on deck, an impatient Bragg leered at Roth and poked at his chest with the captain's stick. 'What do you mean, you don't know where they are?' he spat. 'They're on the ship somewhere. Nothin' can be *lost* on a ship! If you don't find them, you know what'll happen.' Bragg's eyes flicked over to the carpet and Roth gulped. 'Or per'aps I should just *smoke* them out.'

Bragg looked out at the deserted harbour. The sun had almost set. Dutchy was far away at the Circular Quay. He gazed up at the masts, yards and rigging above him.

'Set fire to the ship!' he commanded, his arms opened wide.

Mr Mason and Mr Leer watched aghast as Roth obeyed Bragg's order without question. He picked up a lantern and threw it onto a pile of coiled ropes. It smashed and burst into flames.

At that very moment, the brawl in the mess room spilled out onto the deck. Like monkeys, the *Sobraon* boys scrambled up the masts and along the yards, pelting Bragg and his boys with cutlery they'd brought from the mess room. But some of the *Sobraon* boys who were loyal to Bragg headed up there too, fighting their foes high in the air.

The fire began to take hold, racing across the deck and licking at the masts.

'To the hoses!' yelled the prefects, who had just arrived on deck. They sprang to the pumps that drew water from the sea. More boys joined them, fending off Bragg's thieves as they tried to grab the nozzles.

'Keep pumping!' the prefects yelled, as the flames began creeping up the mainmast.

CHAPTER 17

# THE THREAT OF THE LEYDEN JAR

Fire clawed its way slowly up the mainmast of the *Sobraon* and spread across the yards. Thick black smoke billowed from the ship. All was chaos.

Boys in sailor suits defended the prefects at the pumps. Others stopped mid-scuffle to watch the fire licking higher and higher up the masts. Booted street urchins wrestled with barefooted *Sobraon* boys.

Marion, Walker and Henry reached the deck. They stared in horror as two boys fell noisily into the water. More jumped in after them. Walker was still clutching Marion's net. He tossed it to a group of *Sobraon* boys, who used it to capture a small gang of thieves, manhandle them to the deck and tie them up.

Then—without warning—Marion was tackled from behind by Roth. She fell hard on her knees and cried out. Roth grabbed at her cap and tugged roughly, and Marion's long locks cascaded down her back. The daughter of the captain was unmasked.

'There she is!' shouted several thieves at once, waving at Bragg.

The fighting paused. Bragg's face lit up with a terrifying grin. He stepped forward, ducking under a burning yard close to his head. He was so transfixed by her, he hardly noticed the flames.

Marion watched mesmerised as Bragg approached, his hob-nail boots thudding across the deck.

Suddenly, the prefects at the pumps were successful and great arcs of water exploded from both hoses. Seawater drenched the deck and everyone on it. A cheer went up as the *Sobraon* boys angled the hoses up towards the fire feasting on the masts.

Bragg clicked his fingers, and his boys resumed their fight against the prefects for control of the hoses.

Like the deck, Marion was drenched. She shivered as Bragg towered over her.

'Never far from the other, are you?' Bragg said, addressing

both her and Walker. Bragg glared at Henry, who was behind them. 'If you don't move right now, Edwards, I'll make your right eye match the left.'

Behind Bragg, members of the Forty Thieves got hold of the hoses and directed them away from the flames.

'Go!' Bragg instructed, lunging at Henry.

Henry dodged him just in time and skittered away, the Leyden jar still clutched to his chest.

Bragg turned to Marion. 'You're a bit o' jam, aren't you?' he observed as she knelt on the deck, looking up at him. 'Even in those ridiculous clothes.'

Marion didn't understand what he was saying, but she certainly understood his tone. Walker strained against Roth, who was holding his arms behind his back.

Bragg looked amused. 'Looking for a chivy duel, are we Crosscapel?'

Walker blinked.

'Do you know your mother threatened me again last night? I've invited her to tea tomorrow. But I daresay I'll have a lovelier time than she will. At least it will stop her pestering me about you.' He laughed as he drew his finger across his throat.

Behind Bragg, the *Sobraon* boys had won back control of the hoses and the fire was almost out. Water continued to pour onto the deck. Bragg wriggled his toes in his soggy boots and wrinkled his nose.

Marion looked around. Henry was saying something to Mr Mason, who listened intently. Cradling the Leyden jar in the crook of his bad arm, Henry slipped his good hand into Mr Mason's breast pocket and withdrew a silver whistle. At the same time, a prefect carrying a knife reached the mast where Mr Mason and Mr Leer were tied up, and their ropes fell away. Henry passed the Leyden jar to the prefect, who hid it behind his back.

'My name really *is* Crosscapel?' a dumbfounded Walker asked Bragg. 'You kidnapped me from my mother!' he shouted. 'You made me forget her. You told me she was *dead*.'

Walker broke free from Roth's grip and lurched towards Bragg, just as Mr Mason blew his whistle and cried, '*Sobraon* boys, man the yards!'

The rest of the boys from classes one to six clambered up the masts and along the yards, pulling Mr Mason and the staff up with them.

Walker was wrestling with Bragg when a boom came swinging past carrying two prefects, who scooped Marion and Walker up in one smooth movement.

The only people still standing in the water were Bragg and the members of the Forty Thieves, along with Roth's gang. Everyone else was high up in the rigging. The prefect beside Marion shoved the Leyden jar into her hands.

Bragg looked up at the sailor-suited boys peering down at him. He laughed as he sloshed around in the water on the deck. 'You think you can dangle up there forever? Roth, grab another lantern.'

'Stop!' yelled Marion. 'Move one step and I'll drop this!' She held up the Leyden jar for everyone to see.

At first, there was silence. For most of them, what she was holding was a mystery.

'Mr Bragg!' one of the boys on the deck yelled, his eyes wide. It was the boy who'd made fun of Marion in the schoolroom earlier in the day. 'That's *electric.* If she drops it, we'll all be electrocuted!'

Enraged, Bragg kicked out at the boy nearest him. He slid out of the way just in time.

'Surrender!' a *Sobraon* boy shouted from high up in the rigging, as others hooted and cheered.

'Surrender, Bragg!' came the cry.

But something else was happening on the port side of the ship. Boys craned their heads to see what it was.

'Surrender!' came the call again from the boys sitting comfortably on the yards, swinging their legs.

Bragg peered around, a calculating look on his face.

'An excellent idea, boys,' said a spritely voice from the gangway. It was Mr Fosbery, followed by several police officers.

Fosbery stepped confidently towards Bragg and stood calmly in the water on the deck, surveying the scene before him. 'A Leyden jar, Miss Neitenstein? Ingenious! I remember making one of those at school in my younger days.' He glanced at Bragg. 'It's not dangerous at all in this case,' he said, clamping a hand on Bragg's shoulder. 'You're under arrest!' he growled.

The police officers began rounding up Bragg's thieves, who spat and whined in protest.

'Setting fire to a *school*, Joseph,' Fosbery continued, tut-tutting. 'Even for you, that's a low move.'

The boys watched on from the yards and the rigging, like monkeys watching a tiger hunting on the jungle floor.

While Bragg slumped between two policeman, Fosbery toured the deck. He tapped the soggy Killing Carpet with his foot as though he recognised it, then ambled back to Bragg. 'Do you know how you caught my attention this evening?' Fosbery asked. 'There I was, strolling around Balmain, asking myself this and that on my way back home from the Colonial Secretary's house. I was trying a new block of Mr Tart's latest confectionary—I'm quite the connoisseur, you know—when a distressed lady ran past me, shouting that her son was on the *Sobraon* and the ship was on fire.'

Fosbery paused and looked around him.

'Well, Mr Bragg,' he continued, 'I couldn't ignore a lady in distress, so I inquired further. And what a story she told me! I must admit that when she showed me a letter from Miss Neitenstein telling her that her son had been located after being kidnapped by you some years ago, I was certainly interested.'

Mr Fosbery paused and reached into his pocket for a piece of fudge. In the silence, a scratching sound could be heard below deck, followed by the sound of trotting feet. Jumbo burst through the gap where the quarterdeck doors used to be and launched onto the slippery deck, barking frantically.

With a growl, the dog barrelled into Bragg, sending him flying. Bragg slid through the water and hurtled towards the railing, where Henry stood. Desperate to get away from the snarling dog, Bragg stumbled about as he struggled to gain a foothold, but the *Sobraon* boys pushed him away with their feet.

Henry stuck out his foot to bat Bragg away too but, with a spark of triumph in his eyes, Bragg caught hold of Henry's foot and pushed him hard. His good arm wheeling uselessly, Henry fell backwards, hit his head on the railing and plunged into the sea.

Fosbery pulled Bragg to his feet and snapped handcuffs on his wrists as Jumbo charged over the side of the ship. Several *Sobraon* boys, including Alexander Walker, followed him into the water. Everyone's eyes were on the white foam that marked where they'd dived in.

Walker finally resurfaced, with Jumbo panting beside him. But Henry Edwards was not with them.

# CHAPTER 18

# AN END AND A BEGINNING

*Dear Agnes,*

*Sadly, the boy I mentioned in my last letter—Henry Edwards—never woke up. His limp body was brought up from the ocean floor with a terrible cut on the back of his head. Mr Mason and Alexander Walker shared the task of getting him to the gangway and carrying him back to the deck. It took some time to find him, and they had to dive very deep indeed, but it was too late for poor Henry.*

*He was buried at Rookwood Cemetery this morning as the* Sobraon *band played beside his grave. I have never seen Papa sob before. He stood at the head of the fresh grave, cap in hand. I went to the library after the funeral, but the books reminded me of Henry, so I just sat there and wept.*

*The other* Sobraon *boys had a terrible time coaxing Jumbo out of the water at first, but as soon as his master's body was brought up, pale in the arms of Mr Mason, the dog swam back to the ship in their wake. The loyal hound has not left Henry's hammock, and he continually looks about him, waiting for his master to return. The sight brings many of the boys to tears, and even Norman Roth seems touched by it. He brought the dog a scrap of bread for his supper this evening.*

*Alexander Walker—or should I say Julian Crosscapel—has not been on the ship since his mother came to collect him three days ago. He attended Henry's funeral though in a smart sailor suit, and Mrs Crosscapel was there too. She offered me the reward for finding her son. It has been donated—along with the prefects' pocket money for the next couple of months—to a fund to give Henry a proper gravestone. As he has no parents, there is no one else to do this for him. I can't remember what I said to him when he told me how his father had abandoned him. I hope I was a good friend and comforted him.*

*On the way back to the ship after the funeral, Walker told me the whole sorry tale of Mr Bragg and his mother. It seems that many years ago Mr Bragg tricked Mr Crosscapel into taking out a large loan he would never be able to repay. Walker's father entered into the deal secretly, to protect his wife and young son. But he became ill with worry, as he could not repay what he owed. And then he died.*

*When Bragg found out, animal-like, he threatened Mrs Crosscapel—to whom he showed the paperwork and the letters with her husband's signatures. Grieving for her husband and her son's father, Mrs Crosscapel tried to repay what her husband owed. She was thrifty, but she fell quickly into poverty as she struggled to make payments to the rough, threatening men who arrived at her house demanding money.*

*During this time, Mrs Crosscapel often returned home to find ragged boys and scary men peering at her son through the windows. Once she even stumbled upon a stranger in her house, who told her that Julian was clever for his age. A few days later, when her son was out on the street playing, she observed the same stranger watching from afar. Smart, good at running and climbing, Julian was a perfect fit for the Forty Thieves.*

*Then one day she arrived home and Julian was gone. He had simply disappeared. Frantic, she searched for him every day. She suspected that Bragg had kidnapped her child.*

*Walker was tricked by Bragg into believing his mother was dead, and at that point Bragg had won. Mrs Crosscapel continued to repay her husband's debt, and Bragg had found his best thief. For years, the mother searched for her son, while Walker was fooled into believing that Mr Bragg cared for and cherished him.*

*When Alexander Walker—I mean, Julian Crosscapel!—first arrived on the ship, I did not like him one bit. But I shall always remember his face when he saw me in Sewers Canal and tried to save me. And I was so pleased when we were hiding in the aviary and he told Henry that I can look after myself. I do miss him. I miss them both. Mrs Crosscapel says I may visit her house whenever I like. And I shall!*

*I am starting at my new school tomorrow. Some of the boys have offered to row me to Cockatoo Island and wait with me for the ferry. I must go now.*

*Yours in sorrow &c &c,*

*Marion*

# AUTHOR'S NOTE

Marion Selina Neitenstein lived in Sydney more than a hundred years ago. Other characters in this book—like Marion's parents, Quong Tart, Joseph Bragg, Mr Leer, Mr Mason, Mr Fosbery and Mr Inglis—were real people too. However, I used my imagination to create Alexander Walker, Henry Edwards and other secondary characters, although they are all based on real people I researched.

Marion was born in Sydney, almost 150 years ago. Until she was sixteen she lived on the Nautical School Ship *Sobraon* with her mother and father. The Nautical School Ships were anchored at Cockatoo Island on the Parramatta River. They were boarding schools for poor and homeless boys in

New South Wales. They opened in 1867 and closed in 1911. The first ship was called the *Vernon*, and the *Sobraon* replaced her in 1892.

According to a newspaper report, when Marion was six years old she presented prizes to her father's pupils after an exciting boat race on the harbour. She also appears in photographs of the boys playing on Cockatoo Island. She seems to have been in close contact with her father's pupils.

Marion also loved animals, and her best subject at school was Latin, for which she won a prize at Sydney Girls High School in 1896. In the same year, her father received a promotion and she left the *Sobraon* with her family. They moved to Burwood in Sydney's Inner West. Marion never married. She died in 1968 and was buried beside her parents at Rookwood Necropolis.

In 1896, when Marion left the ship, four of the Nautical School Ship boys wrote her a letter and presented her with a gift. It is impossible for us today to discover why they valued her so much. This book uses a mixture of fiction and nonfiction to fill that gap so that the story of the only girl on the Nautical School Ship *Sobraon* can finally be told.

# GLOSSARY

**&**

| | |
|---|---|
| **&c** | abbreviation for et cetera |

**A**

| | |
|---|---|
| **aft** | rear of a ship or boat |

**B**

| | |
|---|---|
| **bard** | poet |
| **berths** | sleeping spaces, a bed or hammock |
| **bit o' jam** | pretty girl |
| **black maria** | prison van |
| **blackboard** | chalkboard |
| **boom** | long movable beam of wood attached to the mast of a ship |
| **bottle-shouldered** | slumped, round-shouldered |

| | |
|---|---|
| **bow** | front of a ship or boat |

**C**

| | |
|---|---|
| **capital** | good, fine |
| **carousing** | loud, sometimes violent, fun |
| **catarrh** | mucus or snot in the nose and throat |
| **chintz** | fabric with colourful flowered patterns |
| **chivy duel** | a fight with knives |
| **classifieds** | advertisements |
| **claustrophobic** | fear of confined places |
| **confectionary** | sweets, lollies |
| **connoisseur** | expert in or collector of something |
| **copperleaf** | very thin sheets of copper |
| **copperplate** | elegant running writing |
| **coppers** | police officers |
| **corset** | underwear worn by women and girls that constrains the torso |
| **cutters** | small boats with a single mast |

**D**

| | |
|---|---|
| **deportment** | good manners, poise and proper behaviour |

| | |
|---|---|
| **dining saloon** | large, ornate dining room |
| **dive a pocket** | pick a pocket, steal |
| **dockworkers** | people who work at shipyards |
| **drydock** | place where ships are repaired and maintained |

**F**

| | |
|---|---|
| **falling in** | going to |
| **feeling the collar** | feeling the heat on a hot day |
| **filch** | steal |
| **fit-up** | trick |
| **frockcoat** | long coat worn by gentlemen |
| **frogmarching** | pushing someone along while holding their arms behind them |

**G**

| | |
|---|---|
| **garret** | mouth |
| **gawd** | god |
| **gibberish** | unclear speech or writing |
| **gigglemugged** | silly, constantly smiling |
| **grey** | money |

**H**

| | |
|---|---|
| **half-hunter watch** | pocket watch with a glass lid |

| | |
|---|---|
| **hard eggs** | people resistant to change |
| **hatches** | hinged doors leading onto the deck of a ship |
| **have a down** | bear a grudge |
| **hijinks** | noisy fun, such as practical jokes |
| **hullabaloo** | chaos, disturbance |

## I

| | |
|---|---|
| **inkwells** | small containers holding ink for writing |

## J

| | |
|---|---|
| **jolly boat** | small rowboat or dinghy |
| **jugged hare** | stew made from a hare or a rabbit |

## K

| | |
|---|---|
| **knickknacks** | trinkets |

## L

| | |
|---|---|
| **larrikin** | poorly behaved young person |
| **Leyden jar** | a container that stores electrical charge |
| **lifted** | stolen |
| **lionise** | honour, give attention to |
| **lop-eared** | floppy-eared |

| | |
|---|---|
| **lump o' jaw** | talkative person |

**M**

| | |
|---|---|
| **magic lantern** | slide projector |
| **make warm** | punish |
| **man-o-war** | warship |
| **mess room** | room on a ship for recreation and meals |
| **mock turtle soup** | traditional English soup made from calf heads and brains |

**N**

| | |
|---|---|
| **nap the regulars** | earn money from the sale of stolen property |
| **neckerchief** | piece of cloth tied around the neck |

**O**

| | |
|---|---|
| **on the square** | totally honest |
| **opium den** | shop where the drug opium is purchased and smoked |

**P**

| | |
|---|---|
| **parlour** | living room in a house |
| **pennorth of treacle** | charming girl |
| **pockmarked** | disfigured by scars |
| **port** | left side of a ship |
| **portholes** | small round windows in a ship |

| | |
|---|---|
| **pull the string** | manipulate someone |
| **push** | criminal gang |
| **put lights out** | kill someone |

**Q**

| | |
|---|---|
| **quarterdeck** | raised deck behind the mainmast of a ship |
| **quarters** | rooms for personal or private use |

**R**

| | |
|---|---|
| **redding** | watch, pocket watch |
| **ruckus** | loud sometimes violent disturbance |

**S**

| | |
|---|---|
| **sealing wax** | coloured wax used for sealing envelopes and important documents |
| **six foot of tripe** | a large policeman |
| **skylarking** | passing time by joking and messing around |
| **smarts** | understanding, skills and/or knowledge |
| **sneak budge** | shoplift |
| **snuffed it** | died |
| **softie and a noodle** | a hypochondriac |
| **spieler** | swindler, con artist |

| | |
|---|---|
| **stern** | rear section of a ship or boat |
| **street urchins** | homeless children |
| **suffrage** | right to vote in elections |
| **sweets** | cakes, ices, toffee etc. |

**T**

| | |
|---|---|
| **tip** | extra money paid for help, service or assistance |
| **tra, la, la** | rude way to say goodbye |
| **tripe** | nonsense, rubbish |
| **tugboat** | small boat that pulls larger vessels through the water |
| **turncoat** | traitor |

**V**

| | |
|---|---|
| **vagabond** | homeless adult |

**W**

| | |
|---|---|
| **wake** | wave that a boat or ship creates as it moves through the water |

**Y**

| | |
|---|---|
| **yard** | unit of measurement just short of one metre |
| **yards** | spars or masts on a ship to which the sails are attached |

# THE HISTORY OF THE NAUTICAL SCHOOL SHIPS *VERNON* AND *SOBRAON*

## The *Vernon*

From 1866 in New South Wales, you could be arrested if you were under sixteen years old and loitering in public, either because you had no job or were skipping school. Eventually, boys would be brought to the Nautical School Ship *Vernon*. The *Vernon* was a special type of school, called an industrial school. Here, children learned to read and count, if they couldn't already, and some studied subjects like geography and mathematics. They were also taught a trade—usually gardening, tailoring, boot-making or sailing.

After about a year on the *Vernon*, the boys were sent out to the countryside to work until they were eighteen. The youngest boys sent to work were about eight years old, and the oldest were about sixteen years old.

Donald McHenry (11), Joseph Lister (17) and Michael Martin (6) boarded the *Sobraon* between September 1897 and April 1898. Joseph even lied to the admissions board, claiming to be 14, so that he would be allowed to stay on the ship.

Instead of going to the *Vernon*, girls were sent at first to a school in Newcastle. Later, that school moved to Cockatoo Island, before it finally settled in Parramatta. All the children, boys and girls, earned money from their work, which was kept in a bank account that they could access after they turned eighteen. The majority of them worked as farmhands or servants.

Many of these children were orphans, or had parents who were not able (or didn't want) to look after them. People assumed *Vernon* boys were criminals, but this was not true. In fact, for most of the school's history, having a criminal record meant that a boy would not be allowed onboard. New South Wales had separate gaols especially for criminal children, and the *Vernon* was not one of them.

**Captain Mein**

The first captain of the *Vernon* was James Seton Veitch Mein. He had pet monkeys that ran about on the deck of the ship and entertained the boys. While he had good intentions, Captain Mein did not do a very good job as principal of the school. He was very harsh in punishing bad behaviour, often caning students (which was usual for the time) or even flogging them. Under Captain Mein the boys also did not have much time to run around, play with pets or learn to swim. They were exhausted from all the work he set them!

## Captain Neitenstein

Captain Mein died in 1878 and was replaced by Captain Frederick William Neitenstein, Marion's father. Neitenstein was in charge between 1878 and 1896, when he left to become Comptroller-General of Prisons, which meant that he ran New South Wales' gaols. Neitenstein was born in London in 1850, and married his wife (who was also called Marion) in 1879. Their only child, the hero of this book, was born in 1880. The family lived on the ship, in a private apartment, for almost twenty years.

On becoming captain, Neitenstein saw that the school's very busy timetable needed to be changed. He made it so that the boys had a lot more time to play and exercise. He also altered the school rules so that boys were divided up into seven classes, with the top classes being prefects. The lowest class was a punishment class, and those boys had to clean brass work and sweep the ship during play time. Neitenstein's idea was that good behaviour earned a boy entry into the next class, and bad behaviour would see him drop down to the class below. He believed that this was better motivation to be good, than flogging bad boys like Mein had done. Well-behaved boys received extra rewards like access to pets to play with, and got to join the school's sporting clubs. The prefects also received pocket money.

Marion can be seen at the back of this photograph of the boys at play. She is beneath the boys doing gymnastics, wearing a white hat and holding one of the school pets.

Most of the classes had access to the library. Some of the best-behaved boys were given the opportunity to learn an instrument and join the ship's band. The bandmaster was James Francis Bourke, who himself had been a *Vernon* boy.

## The *Sobraon* and Captain Mason

In 1892 the *Vernon* had been so successful that the government bought the *Sobraon* to replace it.

The *Sobraon* was three times bigger than the *Vernon* and could hold more than 300 students at a time. It had a much larger schoolroom and mess room too. Four years later, when Captain Neitenstein got his promotion and moved to Burwood, his lieutenant, William Henry Mason, was made captain. Captain Mason had worked with Neitenstein for a long time, and didn't make many changes to the way the school worked. In 1911 the school was closed, since it was regarded as an old-fashioned way to care for children. Some of the boys were sent to the Mittagong Farm Home, and others started a new school at Mount Penang in Gosford. Here, the boys continued to use *Sobraon* vocabulary: they named their assembly area the 'quarter deck' and labelled their dormitories 'Vernon' and 'Sobraon'.

## Famous *Vernon* and *Sobraon* Boys

The *Vernon* and *Sobraon* had some famous boys on board between 1867 and 1911. Some of the boys are celebrities because they became feared criminals in Sydney. There was John Sleigh, who became a dangerous bushranger (but used his skills in swimming, which he learned as a boy, to save a man who was drowning), and Tommy Cox who was a boxer and violent push-leader. In 1889, Joseph Bragg's own son was taken on board, and Bragg was very angry about it. But there were also some well-behaved boys. The most famous was Bernard Bede 'B. B.' Kieran, who was a world champion swimmer and was a member of the *Sobraon*'s swimming club for a long time.

## The Rocks

In the late nineteenth century, The Rocks was regarded by many as a fearsome place. Some people who lived in The Rocks were quite poor, and they had a reputation for heavy drinking, gambling and crime. It was a place where new immigrants—particularly Irish and Chinese—tended to settle, and as a result the neighbourhood would have been filled with all kinds of different foods and customs. Some parts of The Rocks were certainly slums—dirty places filled with disease and poor hygiene. Other parts, however, contained well-kept, safe homes filled with silver tea sets, books and other nice things owned by the working classes. One of the gangs or 'pushes' that operated in The Rocks was called the Argyle Cut Push, named after a large hole in the rock face at Argyle Street.

S
S

## Quong Tart

Mei Quong Tart was born in the Canton Province, China, in 1850. As a boy he came to Australia with his uncle in order to mine for gold at Braidwood. In the early 1880s, he travelled to Sydney and opened a small shop that sold Chinese silks and tea. His tea became so popular that he decided to open a chain of cafes across Sydney. The tearooms were very popular places to dine: they were beautiful spaces filled with indoor plants and fish ponds. Tart was also very charitable, often throwing parties for poor or neglected children in 'child-saving' institutions, such as the *Vernon* and *Sobraon*. He lived with his large family in Ashfield, and died in 1903 when his office was robbed and he sustained serious injuries.

# BIBLIOGRAPHY


**Non-fiction**

Luke, Sarah, *Like a Wicked Noah's Ark: The Nautical School Ships Vernon & Sobraon*, North Melbourne: Arcadia, 2020

Ramsland, John, *Children of the Back Lanes: Destitute and Neglected Children in Colonial New South Wales*, Sydney: NSW University Press, 1986

**Fiction**

Ferres, Arthur, 'Jim the Vernon Boy', *His Cousin the Wallaby, and Three Other Australian Stories*, Melbourne: George Robertson, 1896

Lawson, Henry, 'Captain of the Push', *Verses, Popular and Humorous*, Sydney: Angus and Robertson, 1900

Park, Ruth, *Playing Beatie Bow*, West Melbourne: Nelson, 1980

Paterson, Banjo, 'In Push Society', *An Outback Marriage*, Sydney: Angus and Robertson, 1906

Turner, Ethel, *Seven Little Australians*, Melbourne: Ward, Lock and Bowden, 1894

# IMAGE CREDITS

Page 190: Portraits of Sobraon boys from MHNSW-StAC: NRS-3902 *Entrance Books [Industrial Schools Branch]*, Museum of History NSW

Page 192: MHNSW-StAC: NRS-4481-2-[4/8664]-1615 *Naval Officers and Cadets N.S.S. [Nautical School Ship] Sobraon, Sydney*, Museum of History NSW

Page 193: MHNSW-StAC: NRS-4481-2-[4/8624]-809 *Recreation Ground N.S.S. [Nautical School Ship] Sobraon, Sydney*, Museum of History NSW

Page 194: MHNSW-StAC: NRS-4481-2-[4/8665]-1618 *Boy Seamen at Divisions N.S.S. [Nautical School Ship] Sobraon, Sydney*, Museum of History NSW

Page 195: MHNSW-StAC: NRS-4481-2-[4/8624]-807 *The School Room N.S.S. [Nautical School Ship] Sobraon, Sydney*, Museum of History NSW

Page 196 & back cover (left): MHNSW-StAC: NRS-4481-3-[7/16268]-St1095 *Sobraon Near Cockatoo Island N.S.S. [Nautical School Ship]*, Museum of History NSW

Page 198: MHNSW-StAC: NRS-4481-2-[4/8665]-1627 *Swimming Instruction N.S.S. [Nautical School Ship] Sobraon, Sydney*, Museum of History NSW

Page 199: Sir William Johnson and Elliot Johnson, *Argyle Cut, Sydney*, 1900, nla.cat-vn2427228, National Library of Australia

Page 200: George McCredie, *Views Taken during Cleansing Operations, Quarantine Area, Sydney*, 1900, PX*D 95, Mitchell Library, State Library of New South Wales

Page 202: Tesla Studios, *Portrait of Quong Tart*, c.1900s, nla.cat-vn89564, National Library of Australia

Back cover (middle): MHNSW-StAC: NRS-4481-2-[4/8665]-1628 *Library N.S.S. [Nautical School Ship] Sobraon, Sydney*, Museum of History NSW

Back cover (right): Charles Kerry, *King Street, Sydney, New South Wales*, c.1880s, nla.cat-vn6101231, National Library of Australia